GREED AND VENGEANCE

GEORGE M. GOODWIN

For information contact: info@outlawspublishing.com

Cover Art by Michael Thomas

Cover Design: Outlaws Publishing

Published by Outlaws Publishing

July 2024

10 9 8 7 6 5 4 3 2 1

CHAPTER ONE

Greed

According to what I'd been told. I was born in the middle of the night on August 12th in the year of 1842. My parents' names were Travis and Bridget Rayburn. Born on a farm just outside of Evansville Indiana, farm country. My mother and father having come from England. Before he and Mother married, he had five acres of land next to his father's. Between the two of them, they barely got by.

At the age of twenty, my father had inherited five hundred dollars when his uncle, a businessman in London, had died. Shortly after that, he and my mother were married. After much talking to others and to each other about it they decided to come to the colonies. Nothing against their homeland. My father simply had dreams bigger than what land available there could give him. It cost him nearly half of his five hundred dollars just for their ship passage.

After arriving in New York, he set about asking questions of everybody he met about the best farm land. More than a few had pointed him to Indiana. In New York, he bought a second hand wagon, and a pair of mules. A good rifle and what supplies they would need for a time and they set out. In his pocket, he still carried a little over a hundred dollars of what he'd left England with. In Indiana, they bought two hundred acres of the best land he'd ever seen for fifty cents an acre and half of his first year crop.

1

Of course the land had never been plowed and he was sure there would be room to improve it. I was the first child born to them, but their hope was to have more sons, that we may all work the land together. To take care of it and in return it would take care of us for all of our lives. I was named Daniel. Named for father's uncle who had made this possible. Three years later, my brother Charles was born. Then Emmet came along in 1845, followed by Henry in '47 and a daughter who died when only a few days old. Finally Matthew, the youngest in 1851. As our father had hoped when each of us reached the age and size for it we all began helping with the farming. It did well for a good number of years too. Supplying all we needed and a good amount to be sold in Evansville. Leastways up until 1861.

That was the year the war between the states started up. From its beginning Charlie, Emmet and myself had joined the Union Army. In '63, at the age of sixteen, Henry had joined as well although none of us knew about it until the wars end. It was then too that we learned who made it home.

2

Charlie had been in Ohio at the time of Lee's surrender and was the first of us to make it back home. There he found that our pa had died while out plowing the spring before our return. Matt was a boy of fourteen at the time and doing his best to take care of Mother, himself and the farm.

One by one over the next month, the rest of us made it home too. Mother told us often how proud our father had been of his five tall, hard-working sons and for fighting for their country. For the next two years we honestly tried to bring the farm back to what we remembered it being while growing up, but things had changed too much it seemed. The war for one and working without Pa there to lead us was another. We found that we just didn't have the same heart for it anymore.

Maybe the war had changed us too.

Then Mother caught the cold and died in the winter of '67. We buried her beside Pa in what was to be our family cemetery. The two of them had been together since they were little more than children themselves and we saw no reason to change that now. After her death, we boys talked much among ourselves and all of us agreed that we'd sell the farm, take what money we got and go west. Still intending to stay together as a family. With no heart for farming anymore, we considered ranching. Pa had said gold prospecting was too iffy.

So it was that in the spring of '68 with the farm sold and a tidy sum in our pockets, the five of us saddled up and headed west. There we hoped not only to make a go of ranching, but to hopefully in time marry and have families of our own.

3

During the war, both Henry and I had been stationed in Kansas for a spell, at different times. Henry had been a courier during the war. Relaying battle plans and maps from one general to another. My job had been a little different. My troop had been sent to Lawrence Kansas. We went there shortly after William Quantrill and his raiders had seized and burned most of it and killed some one hundred and eighty civilians. We went there with one order only to track down and kill any man that had rode with Quantrill in that raid. In our search for them I had seen those wide open and mostly flat lands and now thought of it as a good place for a ranch. We agreed that would be where we looked first. Surely, we figured Texas had enough cattle ranches already. We knew we had to move quickly though.

Since wars end, we had seen several wagons loaded and headed west. Some of those men having seen the same land that Henry and I had. After several months of looking, we found what we wanted.

Close to a six hundred acres of grassland with a good sized stream running almost dead center of it from north to south.

It showed no signs of improvement or anyone holding claim to it, so in the early summer of 1869 we settled there. We began at once cutting trees from a rather large forest just west of where we intended to build our house. Dodge City, we found was about thirty miles west of our land.

4

Wichita was a hundred and forty miles back to the east. Needless to say we would be doing our business in Dodge City. We rode in together that first time and split up, each having things to find and buy. A wagon, along with axes, ropes and tools needed for building. We would, also, lay in some supply of coffee, flour and other such goods that couldn't be had from hunting or growing.

What coffee we'd left Evansville with was gone the day before we stopped on the property. We, also, asked around about cattle for sale; short of driving a herd in from some great distance. After all, we were farm boys, not cowboys and had a lot to learn before driving a herd any distance. Several people told us to check with the ranch just east of us.

"Big ranch," they said, "been there for several years now. Called the double 'D'."

"In fact," one man told Charlie, he was surprised the owner of it, David Douglas hadn't already took it as part of his own. "I guess he's just making do with that measly two thousand acres he has already," the man said.

"Two thousand acres?" said Charlie. "Heck that's bigger than all of Dodge City."

"You're right about that," the man told him, "but he can afford it. Got himself some big shot money backers over in England. Least ways that's what I've heard."

5

We were able to get all we needed on that trip except for the cattle and we headed home. As we were all still single men, we would first build one large bunkhouse, big enough for us all. Next, we built a barn with stalls enough for our horses and several more. We would add even more to it later, if all went well. The creek that ran through the ranch was fast and clear, so there was no need of a well.

For a while then; what days we weren't working on the bunkhouse or barn, we spent riding our boundaries getting a feel of the land or hunting in or near the forest. All of our lives we had been taught to work together, so there were few things that had to be discussed more than what somebody's idea was. Arguing among ourselves was one thing our father would not stand for. By the end of the third month, we were sleeping indoors, as were our horses and several things had been done to better our range. Over supper one night we talked about it and decided it was time to buy cattle. Taking Matt along with me, we rode over to the Douglas Ranch.

Three miles east of our turn off we saw a well-worn path leading off toward the north. Following it we found his house on the western side of the property. Not more than two miles or so from our line.

6

"Lord almighty, what a house," said Matt, as we rode in. At least four times bigger than our bunkhouse with a barn nearly as big as the house. A cowboy stood near the front steps when we rode in and we told him we were looking for Mr. Douglas and why.

He disappeared into the house, but was soon back. Bringing word that his boss had asked that we come in. We knocked the dust off our clothes as best we could and followed him inside. As grand as the house was outside, the inside was much the same. Matt nor myself had ever seen glass window panes. The farm house we grew up in had board shutters.

Large cloth rugs were on most of the floors that we could see through open doorways. A huge staircase just inside the front door went up to what we assumed was the bedrooms. After a few minutes. the cowboy led us down a long hallway and knocked at a large door.

"Come in," we heard from the other side.

That room was plain compared to what we'd seen so far with the exception of a large ornate desk and a great bearskin for a rug.

A small man rose from behind the desk as we entered. He came around the desk with his hand out to shake. "Welcome to the double 'D'," he said, "I'm David Douglas."

He shook my hand and then Matt's. I told him our names and what it was we wished to see him about.

"So we're neighbors?" he said. "You know I've thought several times of taking in that range myself," he told us. "Just never got around to it. I guess now I never will."

7

He asked where we were from and I told him about growing up farming back in Indiana and about it being just the five of us brothers now.

"That makes it easier," he said. "Sometimes it's hard to find enough hands around here. Most cowboys are a drifting lot. How many head were you looking to buy?" he asked.

"Well Sir," I told him, "I'm not so sure what the land will support."

"Personally, I like one head per two acres," Douglas told me, "but under normal conditions, an acre a head is fine." He said something about his manners, then and asked if we'd like a drink.

We both shook our heads no. "Never had a taste for it," I told him. "Our pa wasn't a drinking man, so we was never around it growing up I guess."

"Probably a good thing," he said. "Some men do okay with it, but I've known others who let it get the best of them. Tell you what, I've got two hundred and fifty head of young stock. Mostly all heifers. but with a few young bulls. More breeders than I need. I was just about to make a drive with them, but since you need them here and now to get you started, I'll let you have those for ten dollars a head. A proven bull will cost you another fifty though."

Seemed fair enough to me and looking at Matt, he nodded his agreement.

I counted out two thousand five hundred and fifty dollars.

Douglas said, "now don't throw yourself short. Be a while before you're ready for your first drive. I don't know how you're fixed for money, but I'd be glad to take half now and a marker for the rest until your first drive."

"Thank you Sir," I told him, "but Pa had never liked being indebted to nobody and I feel the same way. I appreciate the offer, but I'd as soon pay as I go."

"Nothing wrong with that either," said Douglas. He went around behind the desk and made out a paper on the cattle and what brand they now wore. "You'll need that when you take to them to sale," he told me. "That proves you came by them honest. Not that we have near the rustling problem here that they do down in Texas, but it's safer this way."

We shook hands again and he asked me to give him a day or two to cut them out and he'd have his men drive them over.

8

As Matt and I rode away, I told him I thought this man would be a good neighbor to have. Matt agreed that he was sure helpful about how many we should start with and all and then offered credit and him not even knowing us. True to his word, the second day after our visit, his men pushed the herd across onto our range.

One of them told me we'd have to watch 'em a few days as they would try to head back. "They were born here on the ranch, it's home to them," he said.

He wasn't wrong about that.

9

For a solid week we were all constantly driving them back away from the line.

"Well gentlemen," I told them over supper a few days after the cattle arrived, "we are now ranchers."

"Seems strange doesn't it," said Emmet, "how we sold the farm back home for ten thousand dollars. Then we get out here and give nothing at all for this land."

"Not exactly," I told him. "Pa got that farmland back there for nearly nothing when he and Mother first moved onto it. The difference is, he improved on it for years, clearing and planting. Don't you remember the stone boats full of rocks we dug up and removed with every plowing?" I asked him. "Pa made that land worth something and we'll do the same with this land. Make a good showing with our ranch and in twenty years or so we can name our price for it."

"Or could," said Charlie, "if we was ever to decide to sell.'"

"I see what you mean," said Emmet.

By the spring of '73, we had more cattle than the land could support, so we began planning a drive to the railhead in Kansas City Missouri. We would keep about half the cattle we'd bought from Mr. Douglas and sell the others along with most of what had been born there on the ranch. I hoped the five of us could drive three hundred head for some three hundred miles. While we'd all became pretty good cowboys in my book, this would be our first drive.

10

I rode over to talk with Mr. Douglas about the drive.

He told me the best route or at least the one he used himself. Then he caught me by surprise. He asked if I'd be interested in selling out.

"Selling out?" I said. "We're just now getting started Sir."

"Cattle are a lot of trouble most of the time," he said. "I thought maybe you boys were ready to sell your cattle and go back to farming by now."

I told him, "thanks, but no."

Over the next two weeks, we outfitted the wagon with a top and turned it into our chuck wagon.

"We'll take turns being cowboy and cook," I told them.

The day before we were to leave, we rode to Dodge City for enough supplies to see us to Wichita and restock there. The owner of the general store was something of a talker and I was telling him this would be our first drive. "I guess you heard about your neighbor?" he said.

"Don't guess so," I told him.

"Seems like his money men in England turned loose of some more. Douglas bought out the ranch to the east of his place and tried to get the one north of him. I tell you, I look any day now for 'em to change the name of Dodge City to Douglasville or something."

"Tried to buy me out too," I told him.

"Offered or pressured?" he asked me.

"No, just a friendly offer," I told him.

"For now anyway," said the store man.

On the way home, I told the others what he'd said. I'd already told them about Douglas's offer to me when I'd rode over there.

"How much land and how many cattle is enough?" asked Henry.

"No amount for some people," I told him. "Greed knows no bounds for some men. I just want enough to make life a little easier. Not that we're really hurting right now to be honest. Of course if and when any of us marries, it'll mean building more houses. Can't very well move your new wife into a bunkhouse full of brothers."

11

We all laughed about it, but it was the truth.

"You have to at least meet a girl before you worry about that." said Henry.

We hardly ever even come to town. Much less take time to meet any girls. We rode on for a minute not talking.

Then I said, "I think when this drive is over, we need to change that. Say one weekend a month, we take off and go into Dodge. Have a meal one of us didn't have to cook. Maybe stay in the hotel even. Move around town some and see if there are any single women there."

Back in Dodge, I'd hired two out of work cowboys to stay and take care of things at the ranch while we was gone on the drive.

"Easy wages, if nothing bad happens," I told them.

"Seems something bad always happens when you're dealing with cattle," replied the one called Pete.

The other one was called Fencepost and it wasn't hard to figure out why looking at him. At six foot one myself, I had to look up to talk to him eye to eye, but he was the same size from his hat to his heels.

When the herd we was taking came to their feet around five we didn't give em time to be argue. We quickly moved 'em out before they changed their minds.

Our first lesson came quick. We found out that a herd moved about a third as fast as a man on a horse at a steady walk. That is, if one of them didn't decide it was going back home. Then it was all a horse and rider could do to chase it down and change its mind. We pushed from daylight to nearly dark every day and it still took the better part of five days to reach Wichita.

12

Our next stop from there would be El Dorado, if it was needed. According to what I was told, it was only around thirty miles north-east of Wichita. If supplies were still okay, we'd ride right on past. We did just that too and made camp about ten miles north of town. Then another three days to a town called Emporia.

I knew for sure we'd have to stop there and buy more supplies as it was another ninety miles or more before we reached Kansas City Missouri where we were to sell the herd. Until then it was just to ride along. The herd was finally trail broke and gave up on the idea of turning back. Now it was just slow plodding beside or behind the herd all day.

On the fourth day, Matthew asked me, "is that it up ahead Dan. Is that Kansas City?" He was riding chuck today and I had rode up alongside for some water.

"I believe so," I told. "We should reach town around dark." I dropped back then and told the other boys the news.

13

Not bad for a first drive, I told myself. Over three hundred mile and we hadn't lost one steer or had any troubles to speak of. I was proud of us all.

Now I knew for sure we'd never be a farmers again. The man at the stockyard looked the cattle over as we pushed them into a holding corral until they were loaded on the train. As the last few walked in the gate, he climbed down and came over to me.

"I got a count of three hundred even," he said, "that sound right?"

"Yes Sir," I told him.

"Saw a couple of different brands mixed, you got papers on what's not your brand?"

I pulled the bill of sale that Douglas had written from my pocket and handed it to him.

"I can go you twenty-five a head," he said. "Prices are down a little right now, that alright?"

"Sounds good to me," I told him.

He asked if we wanted it in cash. "That or I can wire the money to your closest town. If they have a bank."

"Well, Dodge City hasn't got a bank just yet," I told him. "There's five of us though. All crack shots, I guess we can hold onto the cash we worked so hard for."

He counted out seventy-five hundred dollars and handed it to me as I signed a paper for him.

A month and a half it had taken us, but we made it I thought. *Every drive from now on will get easier and easier as we grow into being cowboys* I thought.

That evening after cleaning up and washing off the trail dust we went to a restaurant. We all wanted a good meal. One that we hadn't cooked.

"We might make cowboys yet," I told them as we sat at the table, "but I don't hold much hope of any of us becoming good cooks."

14

We had the first sit down together at a table meal we'd had in a number of years. Afterward, we rode just back outside of town and made camp. Up with the sun and moving on. The wagon was all there was to slow us down now, but we still got back to the ranch in just over half the time it took us going there.

The two men I'd hired to watch over things had done well. I paid them sixty dollars; the same wages as they would have made riding for a month and asked if they were interested in more work later on.

"Yes Sir, if we ain't done hooked up with another outfit," said Fencepost.

Later in the bunkhouse, I figured what we'd spent on the trip and deducted it from what the herd had brought in Missouri. The rest of it I split five ways among us. Nearly fifteen hundred dollars each.

It was more money than any one of us could ever call his own before. The money from the farm sale had belonged to us all and had bought the ranch, the cattle from Douglas and other things we needed.

"Not bad for our first drive," I told my brothers.

"Pa always said if we'd stick together, we could go far," said Charlie.

Two weeks after we arrived back home, David

Douglas rode up to the house one morning.

I was sitting outside when he rode in.

"Howdy," he said on seeing me.

"Hello," I answered. "What brings you over this way Mr. Douglas?"

"Been thinking about what we talked about a while back?" he said.

"What would that be?" I asked him.

"You remember, about selling me this place," he said.

"Yes Sir, I remember," I told him. "I also remember telling you it wasn't for sale."

"You haven't even heard my best offer yet."

"Don't need to. We like it here. We made some money on that first drive and that makes us like it even more. I heard talk in Dodge that you had bought out the ranches both to your east and north. Surely with all that, our little six hundred acres wouldn't make much difference."

"What did you and your brothers make on that drive, maybe a thousand dollars each?"

15

"Fifteen hundred," I told him.

"Okay fifteen," he said. "Hell, you wouldn't have that if not for the cattle you got from me."

"Bought Mr. Douglas, bought from you. You gave us nothing, but even if you had in order to help us get started, why are you now trying to get rid of us. You already have more land than any other ranch around here. Is it never enough for you?"

He turned away shaking his head, then turned back. "This is my last offer. I'll give each of you boys five thousand dollars cash today to pack up your personal belongings and ride away from here by dark."

"Thank you for the offer, but like I said before, we're not interested."

16

He climbed on his horse like he was trying to drag the poor thing to the ground. He looked at me hard eyed, then before riding out he shouted, "I'm used to getting what I want around here Rayburn and I'll damn sure get this place too!"

"Is that a threat?"

"You take it any damn way you want," he said. "Because that's exactly what I'm gonna do." He spun his horse and charged out of the yard just as the boys were riding in.

"He was in an awful hurry," said Charlie as they stepped down.

I told them what had taken place and what he'd said. Then I added, "maybe I spoke out of turn. I should have asked you boys if you wanted to sell."

They all shook their heads no.

Charlie said, "you know we're all in this together and as the oldest brother, we sort of expected of you to speak for us all Dan."

"You think he meant those threats?" asked Matt.

"I think he's a greedy rich man who's used to getting his way," I told him. "That's a good kind to keep your eyes on. Greed knows no limits."

We saw nothing more of Douglas right away. Life was much the same every day now. Ride the property line, push a few head back here or there toward home, check water and grass conditions and the like.

However, a few nights after the argument with Douglas, Matt woke us up that morning. He was standing in the doorway of the bunkhouse shouting, "FIRE!"

Running outside we could all see flames toward the back side of the ranch. I suddenly felt the wind was in my face at the same time.

17

Then it hit me.

We hadn't had a rain in nearly a month. The grass had already begun to turn dry and brown in places.

"We have to move boys, that fire will push our herd right over the top of us," I told them. We older boys had helped Pa do a controlled burn on sections of the farm years ago, before we plowed. I told Matt to load anything that would hold water on the wagon and go fill them.

"Henry," I said, "go saddle all the horses, but without blankets."

While they went to that task, Emmet, Charlie and me rounded up what grain sacks we could find in the barn, our horse blankets.

I even told him, "grab our own bedroll blankets."

I caught Matt as he was pulling away from the creek and led him where I wanted him. He had put three barrels at the very back of the wagon. When the other boys joined us there, I quickly told them my plan. Taking an axe from the wagon, I put several splits in the sides.

"Drive from the creek to the property line," I told Matt. "Come back and refill quickly and do it again. Stay no less than thirty feet out in front of the fire line. Don't drive too fast, give it time to soak things a little."

The rest of us dipped our blankets in the remaining

barrels. We rode around behind the blaze and beat out anything that was still burning after the wagon had passed. It didn't take long before we had the fire was completely out. Maybe three hundred feet from the barn and the bunkhouse. Between the speed we were working and the heat though, it seemed like it had taken forever.

18

By the light of morning we saw that most of the herd had charged across the creek with only a few stopping in the ranch yard.

Those few now lingered around the yard grazing. Between us, there were some blisters and scraps, but nothing serious.

"We came out a lot better than I thought we would," I told the others.

"Wonder what started it in the first place?" asked Emmet.

After a minute I said, "maybe heat lightning. "Maybe," I said under my breath.

After breakfast I saddled my horse and rode the line between our place and Douglas's. Other than a patch here or there, I noticed that fire held pretty much a straight line. I knew then that Douglas had set that blaze after soaking a line right down the boundary himself. I knew, but had no way to prove it, so I said nothing about it to the boys.

At dinnertime, I was back at the ranch and told them we had a problem.

"Fires out," said Matt.

"Yes I know," I told him, "but we now have barely half the grazing land we had. Take a while for new grass to come up. I had figured to wait until spring next year to make another drive, but the land won't support the number of cattle we have now. I'm afraid we'll have to make another drive. That or stand a chance of losing them all."

19

No bigger a place than we were, we needed no roundup to brand anything not branded. We kept them branded a few along as they reached a certain age. We started at once preparing for a drive.

I took the wagon into Dodge for supplies alone this time. I was standing in the general store when I overheard two men in there talking. "I guess ole Douglas figured a way to get that ranch on this side of him after all" said one.

"Yeah, if you can't buy 'em out, burn 'em out," said the other man. "That or make 'em just disappear like that feller north of him did. I reckon about now them sodbusters are wishing they'd a took that money. "

"They should have and rode back east where they come from," said the first man.

"I reckon not!" I said very loud.

Both heads spun in my direction.

"That's my ranch you're talking about," I said. Reaching to my side, I took the loop off my pistol. "You boys know something or are you just making things up as you go along. Maybe the three of us need to walk over to the sheriff's office and talk to him."

"Aw shucks Mister, we was just running off at the mouth. We don't care for Douglas ourselves, but I ain't about to go to the law on him for anything that I ain't seen him do with my own eyes. Only then, if I'm ready to ride away from here."

They left and I finished giving the clerk the list of goods. "Anybody get hurt?" he asked me.

"No," I said, "just lost about half my grass or more. That's what this is," I told him pointing at the things on the counter. "We have to make a drive before I was really planning to."

While we were carrying the things to the wagon, I saw Fencepost across the street and shouted for him to walk over. "I was just about to start hunting you and Pete," I told him. "Wanted to see if you boys wanted to make them easy wages again?"

"Shucks Mr. Rayburn, Pete was kilt in a saloon fight about a week ago and I'm working for a little ranch west of here."

We shook and I wished him luck with his new job.

20

With the supplies loaded, I paid Clyde and headed for home. All the way there it kept gnawing at me that if we all left like last time, we'd have nothing when we got back. Whether they'd say so to the law or not, I knew what they said was true. When I got back to the ranch. I rounded up the boys and told them what I suspected about Douglas and that fire. "I think if we all go, he'll say we abandoned the place and lay claim to it, or at least burn it down. I figure on staying here to make sure that don't happen. Stop in Wichita for supplies, like last time and ask around about another rider; if you feel you need one. Offer him thirty dollars a month, rider's wages and a hot meal every day."

So it was that three days later I watched as my brothers moved the herd out.

21

Once again; they were headed to Kansas City. I had a strange feeling in my gut that something was going to go wrong. Only, not with them, but with me being here alone. If Douglas had helped that other ranch owner north of here disappear like I'd heard, what was to stop him from doing the same to me here alone. I couldn't stay awake night and day.

To make matters worse, a few days after the boys left, I went to climb over the rail into the corral and a rail broke. It threw me backward and caught my leg between the rail that broke and a lower one. It took me a little while to pull myself upright using the top rail. Finally, I got out of that mess only to find it had twisted my knee and hip badly. To the point that I could barely make it into the bunkhouse.

By nightfall, my knee was swelled to twice its normal size. I put a pan of water on the heater and later soaked a rag in the hot water and wrapped it around the knee. That night, laying in my bunk I couldn't remember ever feeling so alone. All my life, my brothers had been there at home and in the army, I was surrounded by other soldiers. Slowly, my leg healed and I could get back in my saddle again. Riding to the creek for water, I found our fast flowing creek was now barely more than a trickle. "Water could wait," I told myself. I trailed along beside the creek all the way to the north side of our range. What lay beyond I didn't know because we'd never explored past our boundary. I was able to ride about two hundred yards before it became too rough for old Gus. It was the opposite of our land to say the least.

22

It became very rocky and had great snarls of vines running everywhere. Tying Gus, I took out on foot. Walking, I soon found the area also had some holes. *Just the right size for stepping in and breaking a leg* I thought, but still carefully I continued.

Three quarters of a mile there about up the creek, I found a dam made from piling up rocks across the creek. Now a few rocks and you'd call them wash downs. These would be scattered though, not a straight line of them running bank to bank no way.

Three hours later, the creek was flowing normally again.

Douglas hadn't done this I told myself. He may have paid it done though. I had a hard time moving some of those rocks myself. That little man could not have done it alone. I had saw these same tactics while in the army. The Confederate soldiers believed that the more difficult you made life for your enemy, the less they felt like fighting.

I remembered one time when they had snuck up and set a circle of fire around our camp in the middle of the night. No one was hurt, but nobody got any sleep once it was put out either. We lost five men in a skirmish later that day. I wondered now if Douglas had been in the Confederate Army.

23

"Well if he was; he should remember who won the war in spite of those tactics. So will I," I said out loud.

When I got back to the ranch, I found the bunkhouse in shambles. It looked like it had been hit by cannon fire. As I straightened things up, I wondered if he was doing this same kind of thing to the boys.

When a month had passed and they weren't back, I became worried. I rode into Dodge City in hopes they had sent me a wire. Nothing, but as I left the telegraph office, I heard somebody call my name. Turning, I saw the sheriff walking toward me. My heart sank.

"Are you Daniel Rayburn?" he asked, as he drew close to me.

"Yes Sir," I told him.

"My name's Clifford Banks," he said. "I'm the sheriff here. Could you come over to my office before you leave town?"

"Yes Sir," I said, "I'll be glad to come over right now." I untied my horse and walked him the short distance to the sheriff's office. I sat down in a chair across the desk from the sheriff, trying to stay calm.

"Mr. Rayburn," he said, "I have news of your brothers."

"Are they okay?" I remember asking.

"If you mean alive, yes, they are," he said.

Relief flooded over me. Maybe too soon.

"Mr. Rayburn, they are alive," he said, "but I got this telegraph from the sheriff of El Dorado. They have been arrested for the robbery and murder of two men."

"No sir," I told him, "the older three may have killed someone if it was self-defense. Sir, my youngest brother has never even carried a pistol. Where are they being held?" I asked him.

"That's the thing," he said. "Supposedly the murder took place in Kansas City, Missouri, but they weren't caught there."

"So where were they caught?" I asked him.

"According to the wire I received, Charles Rayburn and Matthew Rayburn were arrested in Emporia, here in Kansas. Henry Rayburn in El Dorado and Emmet Rayburn in Wichita. What was it your brothers were doing in Kansas City?" he asked.

24

"They pushed a small herd of cattle there to the stockyard to sale," I told him. "Sheriff Banks, can you tell me who it was that made this claim?"

He called the names of two men I'd never heard before. "They claim to have seen your brothers shoot two men down in cold blood."

"Then go through their pockets and saddle bags." The only thing I could think of was Douglas. "Sheriff Banks, can I tell you what has been going on in the last few months at my ranch?"

"Certainly," he said. "I don't know that it could help your brothers, but you can tell me."

"First, do you know the name David Douglas?" I asked him.

"I don't know him personal," he said, "but I do know the name. I believe he owns a ranch near yours, does he not?"

"Yes, he does," I told him.

I started with the first time Douglas ask me about selling our place to him, then the later threats he made. Next, I told him about the fire.

25

How it had not moved over onto his range at all, as if it had been watered, but burned ours in a straight line from back to front of the ranch. Finally, I told him about the creek suddenly damming itself up.

"So you think this is something he has planned?" the sheriff asked me.

"I can't help but believe that," I told him. "Sir, just before my brothers left on this drive right here at the general store, I overheard two men talking about how Douglas had burned us out. Also, they mentioned how the ranch owner to his north had suddenly disappeared after refusing to sell out to him."

"I must say," said Banks, "I've heard some rather disturbing things about the man, but nothing that would warrant having a U.S. Marshal come out to investigate. I myself have no authority outside the city limits of Dodge you understand."

"Yes sir I do understand and I'm sure it sounds like I'm just trying to take up for my brothers, but it's not just my word. I feel certain the store owner heard them same as I did. Do you know when or where their trials will be held?"

He shook his head no. "All I know is what I read you from the wire. I'm afraid you'll have to go to those towns yourself to find out more. I will talk to Clyde over at the store though."

"Sheriff, if I leave my ranch to go there, as sure as day, he will claim we abandoned the place and take it over."

"I have a friend here in town, a retired judge," he said. "I'll have him file papers to stop anything like that from happening until you have a chance to go see your brothers. You have my word on that."

"Don't know what to do with the rest of my cattle," I said. "Afraid they'll just wander off without somebody there to stop them."

"Got a few loafers around here I could send over if you'd be willing to pay 'em a little," he said.

"Thank you very much Sheriff," I told him and left.

26

I rode back to the ranch as fast as was possible. It was dark when I got there, but I put together what things I needed to pull out in the morning. I was about to lay down for a little while when I thought about the boys' money from our first sale. Didn't take me long to find each of their hiding places. We'd all been taught by Pa that only a fool carried more money on his person than he was apt to need. I wrapped it up along with my own in a cloth and dumping out my coffee, I put it in the bottom of the bag. Then I dumped the coffee back on top of it. I didn't know if it would help me get them out, but I had to try. *No I had to do. I knew this was either all set up by Douglas or somebody had made a bad mistake.* No way, them boys killed or robbed anybody. Although some of them had served in the war as I had and done what was needed, none of them were murderers or thieves.

27

CHAPTER TWO

Injustice

All was quiet for the rest of the night and by good daylight, I was saddled and ready to ride. Suddenly, I remembered what Banks had told me. I wrote a note just in case the heriff did send somebody over to watch the place, for them to make themselves at home and I'd settle up money wise with them when I got back.

On the morning of the third day, I rode up in front of the sheriff's office in Wichita. I went in and told them who I was and that I needed to see my brother Emmet Rayburn.

Making me leave my pistol at the desk, a deputy led me to a cell in the back. Emmet was pacing the floor and looked like he hadn't slept for days. When he turned and saw me, he came at once to the bars.

"You okay?" I asked him.

"Except for being in here," he said.

I told him what Banks had told me and that was all I knew for now. "Can you tell me what happened?" I asked him.

"The drive up was fine all the way there," he said. "No problems at all with the cattle or the wagon. Just like the first time. After we got there, we went and sold the cattle, then went and had a meal at that same place that we did before," said Emmet. "When we was finished we rode out and camped in nearly the same spot as we did before."

28

"The next day, we made maybe another forty miles toward home and camped again, by then, we were no more than thirty miles from Emporia. We probably could have rode on that day and now I wish we had, but we decided to camp again and ride in the following morning. We were needing a few supplies to make it back to the ranch. That next morning, me and Henry was already in the saddle waiting for Charlie and Matt to hitch the wagon when all at once somebody shouted. "don't move! said they was a sheriff's posse. Several of them came into camp with guns drawn and told us we was under arrest for murder and to drop our weapons. When Matt said he didn't carry one, two men jumped him and wrestled him to the ground. Charlie started toward them and all I could think about was how would you know what had happened to us. So I spurred my horse and Henry did the same, right behind me. For a minute there I thought we was dead for sure."

"Lead was flying all around us until we made some distance. Brother, don't think us cowards for running, but we thought sure it was a robbery and that if so they'd kill us all. I thought maybe somebody had saw the stock man pay us for the cattle you know. Then they followed us far enough from Kansas City to rob us so that nobody would suspect them."

29

"After a couple of miles, we noticed that nobody was chasing us, so we stopped and warily rode back to where we had been camped. We was both afraid we was going to find Charlie and Matt dead, but there wasn't nobody or nothing there. They were gone, the horses, wagon everything was gone. Hell, the ashes from our fire was even gone or scattered. "

"We didn't know what to think, but we knew we had to come for you as quick as we could. Our horses was wore slam out by the time we reached El Dorado, so we rode into town. We was hoping to buy some fresh horses, but before we was through making the deal on them six or seven men stormed into the livery. I hadn't taken my saddle off of my horse yet, so I jumped on and went out the back door. They caught or killed Henry though."

"Okay, first off, Henry's alive," I told him. "Secondly, I know none of you are cowards. Charlie and Matt are alive too. They're in jail in Emporia and Henry in El Dorado. You here."

"What's it all about?" Emmet asked me.

"I was hoping you could tell me. They claim the four of you killed and robbed two people in Kansas City."

"Killed and robbed somebody?" he repeated. "Dan, we went straight from the stock-yard to the restaurant and from there to where we camped. I don't remember even seeing anybody after we headed out of town."

"Okay Brother," I told him, "just give me time to go see the others." I said nothing to him about what had went on or was going on at the ranch. He had more than enough on him already.

"Don't worry. I told him. "We'll get it straightened out. I'll be back as soon as I can."

30

Out front, I retrieved my pistol and asked the heriff when Emmet's trial would be.

"Can't rightly say," he told me. "The judge ain't even in town just now."

"I'll be back in a few days," I told him and why I had to go. I rode the thirty miles to El Dorado getting there late that evening. I went straight to the jail. The door was locked when I tried to enter.

I knocked and heard a voice on the other side say, "who is it?"

I told him my name and that I was there to see Henry Rayburn. "No visitors after suppertime," said the voice. "Come back in the morning."

There was little else I could do and I had no stomach for food, so I rode to the livery and stabled my horse and paid the man extra to let me sleep there for the night. When morning came, I went back to the jail. As at Wichita, I was led through a door to the cells.

Henry's account of things was the same as Emmet's. Sold the herd, had a meal rode out of town to camp. Just before Emporia they were jumped by the posse. He too had no idea if the others were even alive.

I told him they were and all in jail either in Emporia or in Wichita.

31

"Why not take us all to one jail? I mean we was caught at different places, but why not take us all to one jail?" he asked.

"I have no answer for that myself and have been asking," I told him.

I wondered why too, *if these murders supposedly took place in Kansas City Missouri, why weren't they all taken back there to stand trial. If they claimed to have witnesses to these murders, wouldn't they need to be there where somebody could identify them.*

"Stay tough," I told Henry. "I'm headed to Emporia to see Matt and Charlie and then try to figure out what our next step is. Might be a few days, but I'll be back."

Three days later, I stepped down in front of the sheriff's office in Emporia. I walked in and told the sheriff who I was and that I was there to see my brothers.

Before he stood up, I asked if he could answer a question for me.

"I'll try," he said.

"If the murders my brothers are accused of took place in Kansas City, why have they not been returned there to stand trial?"

"Because I was told to hold 'em here," he said.

"By who?" I ask.

"Judge Parsons and the mayor, they told me."

"By law they should be returned to the place where the crime is supposed to have happened."

"May be," he said, "but I was ordered by my bosses, the judge and the mayor to hold 'em here. You convince them to send your brothers back to Missouri and I'll take 'em there myself friend. Otherwise, they stay right here. Now do you want to see 'em or not?"

"Absolutely," I told him.

32

Charlie was standing at the bars when I went in. "Thought I heard your voice," he said.

Matt was sleeping on a filthy bunk. "He seems to be taking this well," I told Charlie.

"He's some messed up Dan. When they came into our camp, they ordered us to drop our guns. Matt tried telling them he didn't carry one and three of them jumped on him saying that he was lying. I started toward them, but another one pistol-whipped me from behind and I dropped like a rock. They beat him bad Dan. With their fists and it looks like he was hit with a gun butt a couple of times. Henry and Emmet was in the saddle and when they went to working on Matt and me they lit out, coming for you I knew. You being here now says they made too."

"No they didn't," I told him. "They caught Henry in El Dorado when they tried to get some fresh horses and Emmet down in Wichita. They're both in jail too. Somebody wired the sheriff over in Dodge 'bout what was going on. I just happened to ride over there for some things and he saw me on the street. If he hadn't, I wouldn't be here now."

"Dan I swear we didn't do what they claim," he said.

"I know that for a fact Charlie. What I don't know yet is who said you did and why. Nobody will tell me who, so that I can talk to them myself. Guess I won't know until trial."

33

"Dan?" Charlie asked, "you ever seen them build a gallows before a man's trial even starts?"

"Can't say that I have Charlie."

"Well, they've already built one here. Around behind the jail. That sure don't much make a man believe he's gonna get a fair trial," said Charlie.

"I heard what happened from the others, but do you have any ideas. I need to know who it was that pointed you boys out as the killers."

"I have no idea," said Charlie. "We've had no problem with anybody the whole trip."

"Well, I have an idea, but no proof as yet." I said.

"Douglas?" he asked.

"Yes," I told him and went on to tell him about all that had happened after they left the ranch. "Charlie, you boys are going to have to trust me. I can't make this ride back and forth much and try to do anything else to get you freed, but I am trying."

"I know that without you even saying it," said Charlie. "I'll take care of Matt. You go on and do what you need to do to get us out Dan."

"What about the money from the cattle?" I asked him.

"In that little secret place under the seat," he said.

As I went out, I stopped and tried to ask the sheriff a few more questions. A big sandy haired man stepped between me and the sheriff and said, "Friend, the best thing you can do is leave before you wind up back there with your brothers."

I left there and headed the only other logical place to go. Kansas City. Two hard days ride after talking to Charlie, I stood in the office at the stockyard. I told the stock man some of what was going on. How the boys had all been jailed before they made it back home.

"For what?" he asked me. "They sure didn't strike me as a rowdy bunch."

"For the murders here by the stock yard the same day they was in here," I said.

"Murders?" he said. "There was two cowboys shot and killed each other a while after your brothers rode away, but not murdered. I think it was a fight over a saloon girl."

"Are you sure about that?" I asked him.

"Yes sir," he said. "I was still here working on some paperwork. I heard them arguing and shouting at one another and then a few minutes later, I heard the shots. I went and found 'em myself and then I went for the sheriff."

"Would you be willing to swear to that in court?" I

asked him.

"Sure I would," he said. "Ya'll all seem like real good people, be glad to help."

I left there and went to the sheriff's office. I told him all that had happened and his eyes grew bigger as I went.

"And this is supposed to have happened when?" he asked.

I told him and he shook his head.

Then he told me the same story that the stock man had.

"We've had no murder here in nearly a year," he told me.

"So the men that arrested them wasn't your posse?"

"Son I never even heard of you or your brothers until you walked in that door a few minutes ago."

I told him then the problems I was having with Douglas.

"David Douglas?" he asked me. "Arrogant rich fellow."

34

"Yes sir that's him," I said.

"Douglas was banned from using the stock yard here two years ago," he said. "Those riders of his was nothing but trouble every time they drove a herd in. By the next morning, I'd have a cell full of his men. More like gunmen than cowboys. Then Douglas would stomp in here demanding they be released right then, so that they could head for home. Oh he didn't mind paying for whatever damage they'd done at the saloon or wherever. He enjoyed throwing that money of his around. Thought he could buy his men out of anything. Then two years ago, they brought in a herd and one of his men, after the count, called, Fred, the stock man a liar and hit him. I locked him up and wouldn't let him out until he was tried a month later. Douglas himself threatened me and my deputy and I put him out of town at gunpoint and told him to never come back."

"Sheriff, I think he's set this whole thing up and if I'm right, my brothers are about to hang for something that never even happened. My brother in jail in Emporia told me they had already built a gallows and a trial hasn't even been set. I've got to ride."

"What do you aim to do?" he asked.

"Don't rightly know, but I've got to do something."

"Mr. Rayburn I'm sending for a U.S. Marshal."

"Go ahead," I told him, "but he won't get here in time either way, I don't believe. I'm not even sure I'll get back there in time."

35

As I rode back toward Emporia, I told myself I had to keep my head. *Go in there acting a damn fool and you'll be locked up or dead too* I told myself. *Douglas would like that for sure. Make a clean sweep of all of us at once. That was probably his plan anyway and didn't realize until later that I wasn't with them.*

I knew I was too late when I rode in. That gallows Charlie had spoken of, I rode around and looked at myself before riding north. Well, it had already been torn down. I tried to hope that it was because they had been released, but when I got to the sheriff's office, he said "I'm sorry Son. The judge came back to town just after you left and held trial the same day. We had no way to reach you to let you know."

Blood boiled behind my eyes, but I remembered what I'd thought about earlier.

"Where are their things?" I asked the sheriff.

He reached in a drawer and handed me Charlie's pistol and holster.

"What about the wagon they were on when they were arrested?" I asked.

"Posse brought in no wagon," he told me.

"Sheriff, my brothers had just sold a herd of cattle in Kansas City. One of them was carrying around seventy-five hundred dollars and the two you held here were riding in that wagon."

"I never saw it," he said.

I argued no father with him, I had to ride and ride hard for El Dorado. I just hoped I made it in time. I didn't. I was told by the sheriff that Henry had been hanged two days before I got there.

36

I thought about drawing my gun and killing him right there on the spot, but I held it back. I knew something about myself that even my brothers didn't know. My troop during the war had been considered the toughest of all. It was for that reason that we had been sent to Lawrence in search of Quantrill. As the general had put it, you don't use sheep to hunt wolves. Most of my troop, including me, had spent the last six months of the war in a Union prison for conduct unbecoming a soldier. If I didn't make it to Wichita in time to save Emmet from hanging, I was about to give David Douglas a lesson in war. One that none of them involved would survive. Emmet had been hanged the same day as Henry.

37

As I rode toward the ranch, I thought, *there's no justice for the just.* I had a feeling like something inside me had turned black and died. Three armed men came out of the bunkhouse as I rode in and I was just about to fire on them when I recognized Fencepost.

"Mr. Rayburn," he said, "it's good to see you. How are the other boys holding up?"

"They're gone Fence," I told him. "I was too late everywhere I went. They hanged them all."

He talked to the other two men for a minute and then walked in the bunkhouse with me. "Got some coffee on if you'd like some Boss," he said.

"Thanks Fence," I told him. "I could use a cup.

After he brought it over, I said, I"'ll get you boys paid when I finish this."

"Take your time. I sent them boys on home. Thought I'd hang around here a while if you don't mind that is."

As I drank that coffee, it hit me that I hadn't slept since I'd left Kansas City. For that matter, I wasn't sure if I'd even eaten anything. Everything was blurred in my mind.

38

I didn't remember even laying down, but when I woke, it was hours later, dark in fact. I stood up and told Fence I was going to put my horse away.

"Took care of that while you was resting Mr. Dan."

"Thanks Fence. What are you doing here anyway? I thought you was working for some outfit the other side of Dodge City."

"I was 'til Sheriff Banks told me what was going on and I offered to come watch over the place 'til ya'll got back." He stuttered a little on that "ya'll" and I knew he wished he'd not said it.

"Had any problems?"

"Nary a one," he said.

No, why would you I thought. *Douglas thinks he's won.*

"We even found time to patch up a few things around here. Had a board or two loose on the barn wall and a busted rail on the coral."

"I know," I told him, "it broke under me and almost broke my leg."

"I swear it looked like somebody had sawed it nearly in half right where it broke."

"I'm sure it had been." I'd never thought to look

when it happened, but it made sense.

"Mr. Dan, I don't mean to rush you, but I'd like to know if you plan to stay on?"

39

"Haven't had time to think on it yet" I told him.

"Well sir, if you do, I'd like to stay on here with you and help. I'm no gun hand like that bunch of Douglas' men, but I can shoot."

The fourth day after arriving back at the ranch which I didn't call home anymore, simply the ranch. Home had been taken from me with the death of my brothers, my family. That morning, I told Fencepost we would ride to Dodge City. A plan was working in my head, but I needed help with it. Sheriff Banks seemed an honest and sincere man. He had held his word to send somebody to the ranch as he'd told me he would.

I had no plans of asking him to do anything illegal. Just to get some information for me that as a lawman he could, where I could not. I told Fence I needed to talk to the sheriff alone for a few minutes.

"Okay Boss, I'll go have a beer. Been a while anyway."

"That's fine," I told him and reaching in my pocket I counted out a hundred dollars. "Fence pay them other boys for me and yourself too."

He took half of the money and said, "I'd rather you hold on to the rest of that Boss."

"Tell them I said thanks and if I haven't said it yet,

thank you too Fence."

"You bet," he said and walked away across the street to the saloon.

Banks had saw us outside and met me at the door. "Come in Dan, I've been hoping you'd come by. Ed, one of the boys that was over there told me what happened. I'm very sorry to hear about your brothers."

"I'd like to talk to you about that," I told him.

40

Over the next two hours, I told him all that had happened after he brought me the wire that day. "I think we both know who was behind this," I told him. "First, let me ask a question. If somebody was murdered here in Dodge and the killer was later caught somewhere else, wouldn't he be brought back here to stand trial for his crime?"

"It would be the normal thing yes," he said.

"Can you tell me why then, my brothers were accused of murder in Kansas City, Missouri, but tried and hanged in three different cities, not even in the same state. I'll tell you why, because Douglas has no friends or power there and he had them in three different places to keep me riding instead of getting them out. I need your help."

"Well I don't know what help I could be," he said, "but as long as you don't ask me to cross the line, you have it."

"I need names," I told him.

"Names?"

"Yes sir. I need the names of the judges who sentenced them to hang. Those of the sheriffs who held them in their jails and if possible, those of the men in the posse who brought them there."

I told him about the wagon being gone along with the money from the cattle sale. "Nobody between here and there has gave me a straight answer about nothing."

"What are you fixing to do Dan?" he asked me.

41

"The work of the Lord," I told him.

"The work of the Lord?" he said, not understanding.

"The good book says vengeance belongs to the Lord," I told him. "I'm about to help him."

"I can ask around. I may get no farther than you have seeing as how Dodge was in no way connected to the crime, but I'll try."

"I'd appreciate anything you can do."

Next, I went to the general store. I talked to the owner, Mr. Clyde, and he too told me he was sorry to hear about the boys. "I told Sheriff Banks what them fellers said in here that day. Sure wish it would have helped."

"Thanks," I said.

While I was there, I bought a hundred rounds for both my rifle and pistol.

"Expecting some trouble?" asked Clyde.

"More of the same." I paid him and put them in my saddlebag as I went out. I walked over to the saloon and found Fence sitting at the bar.

'You ready to ride?" he asked, when he saw me come in.

"No rush," I told him. "Finish your beer. In fact, I'll

buy you another and have one with you."

As we rode toward the ranch, I said, "Fence you any judge of horses?"

"Good as anybody I guess," he said.

"Know where I can buy some?"

"How many?" You planning to start horse ranching?"

"No, I just need maybe four. I'm about to start doing a lot of riding and old Gus here needs a break."

"That ranch I worked at a while back would sell me some sure thing," he said.

42

I told Fence nothing of what I was about to do. It wasn't that I didn't trust him I just thought it best. What he didn't know he couldn't be forced to tell. A few days later, I sent Fence to buy horses.

While he was gone, I rode out to look the cattle over and noticed the grass was starting to come back up from the burn. The cattle that were left looked good. Another few weeks and they would have twice the grass they had now. Our whole future, mine and the boys had depended on those cows. Now there was no future for them. No wives or children. No home of their own here on the ranch. I wasn't sure there would be one for me either when this was all over. Because that wouldn't be until every man who'd played a part in the senseless deaths of my brothers was dead too. That or I was.

Right now, my plan was to take each one of them from their home or work. Ride them outside of town, find a likely tree and hang them. No trial, no lawyers and only me for a judge.

43

Fence was back the next morning with four of the best looking horses I'd seen in a while. He handed me what money was left from buying them. "Mr. Gregory said to tell you if you needed more or needed some help just to let him know."

"Damn it Fence, that's the kind of men I expected to find out here. People willing to help one another not men like Douglas."

"Yes sir" he said, I believe Mr. Gregory is a good man myself."

44

A week or so later, I opened the door of the bunkhouse one morning to find a small cloth bag laying there. I picked it up and felt of it and could tell there was a folded paper inside. Opening it, I pulled out a large, piece of paper. On it was a list of names and their jobs, nothing as to who had sent it or to whom. Just in case it fell into the wrong hands. *Good, that was for the best* I thought. I walked to the barn and opened it again and read.

William Parsons- Judge- Emporia, Percy Cain- Sheriff-Emporia. Wayne Watkins- Judge- El Dorado, Bill Agar-Sheriff- El Dorado, James Avery-Judge- Wichita, John Sikes-Sheriff-Wichita. Below that written in another column was the names Sam Wilde, Tom Evans, Buck Moore, Mike Smith, Abe Johnson, Jim Shumaker. Riders for David Douglas- Double "D" ranch.

"Well, well," I said to myself. "Dumb enough to use men that could lead right back to you Douglas."

Now would come that riding I'd told Fence I'd be doing. *Closest first* I thought, *Wichita.*

In the last few weeks I'd done something I'd never done before. My hair had grown longer than usual and I hadn't shaved. I doubted with what few times I'd been to Wichita and now looking like this, nobody there would know me. Two days later. I rode that way on a black horse with a circle star brand, Mr. Gregory's and not likely to be known in Wichita.

45

Three evenings later, I checked in at the Wichita Hotel under the name Kent Waters. It was the name of a boy that lived on a neighboring farm when I was a kid. Now I had never been a drinker or even entered a saloon except that day to get Fence, but since being out here, I'd learned that they were much more than just a place to drink. A lot of talking and business deals went on in them as well as the drinking, fighting and sometimes gunfights. First, I put my saddle bags and bedroll in my room. Then I walked over to the closest one. I sat down at the bar and ordered a beer.

"New around here ain't you?" asked the bar tender.

"Yes sir," I told him. "Out here from Ohio. Scouting out land for a ranch. A big one. Not for myself you understand, but for a group of men back east. Planning to pool their money and buy or settle a considerable amount of land. Many ranches around here now?" I asked.

"Couple," he said, "none too close."

"Maybe you could point me toward some unclaimed or for sale land," I said.

"I wouldn't have no idea myself, but if they come in tonight, there's one or two men that might be able to help you."

"Thanks" I told him. I sat at the bar like I was paying

attention to no one, but had my ears peeled to conversations at several tables close behind me. After two beers and three hours, I knew no more than when I 'd came in. Before I left, I told the bartender my name and that I was at the hotel. If those men you mentioned come in later, send them to me," and laid five silver dollars on the bar.

46

That night I did not sleep well at all. I kept thinking about my brothers, but, also, for what I had planned for the men on that list. When I finally did go to sleep, I saw Charlie in my dreams.

"You can't do what you're thinking Dan," he told me. "It would make you no better than them and you are better."

"I aim to avenge your deaths," I told him.

"Then do it like Father would have. Wrap them up in a nice little bundle and turn them over to the law. Remember when we were kids and started having trouble with somebody stealing our chickens among other things. Pa didn't set up and wait for them with his shotgun and kill them. I'll never forget going in the barn that morning and finding those three men hanging from the roof by one leg. Then how he turned them over to the law."

I had forgotten all about that, but Charlie was right. I had to rethink my plans. I had been back from breakfast a short time the next morning, when there was a knock on my door.

"Who's there?"

"Name's Moore," he said, "Buck Moore. The barkeep sent me over here."

I opened the door to find a big sandy haired cowboy

standing there.

"About the land?" I asked him. "Come in, come in."

"No need," he told me. "I just came to tell you there ain't no land around here. Not for sale, nor for claiming."

"Well maybe not right around here, but surely somewhere a little farther west."

"Best thing you can do is go back to wherever you came from," he said.

47

If I find nothing, I certainly will," I told him.

"Don't push it Friend," he said, "bad things happen to people who push around here." He turned without another word and walked away.

"I'll see you~" I said loudly as he went down the hall. *Yes sir, you can bet on that* I said to myself. I didn't believe he knew me, but I remembered him. That was the second time he'd called me friend. He did it in a way that let me know we was anything but friends. Moore, I found out later, not only worked for Douglas, but was ranch foreman of the double D. Meaning, he done nothing without direct orders from Douglas.

Over the next couple of days, I found out that Judge Avery had left town the day after Emmet was hanged. Sheriff Sikes, about a week later and neither had come back.

"Just up and left," the man told me. "Didn't even give us time to elect a new sheriff."

"Say where they was headed?" I asked.

"Don't recall either one saying, but I heard somebody say they went west. I figured California, like so many others."

"Thanks," I told him.

Back in my room, I took out my list and noted what I

had found out. Avery and Sikes, it looked like would take more searching for than I would spend right now. Buck Moore, I knew where to find anytime, the Douglas' ranch.

"On to El Dorado in the morning," I said to myself.

48

As I rode the thirty miles there, I thought a lot about the first drive, with my brothers. Happy that we had all survived the war, and that things were going well with the ranch for all of us.

Henry had been the most peaceful one of us. In fact, it surprised me when I found out he'd even joined the army. They were all good men and deserved far better than what they had gotten by this greedy bunch of snakes.

As with Wichita, I took a room at the hotel using the same alias as before. I may have been followed to see if I used a different name. Besides, the saloons and the general store were good places to pick up information. *It had been so once before* I thought. I first went and had something to eat.

The waitress who brought my food was a young woman about my own age. "I know about everyone in town, so you must be new around here."

I shook my head yes. "Just here on business. Name's Kent Waters."

"Well if you need anything else Mr. Waters, my name is Lily." she said and walked away.

Seems like a nice girl I thought, *pretty too.*

I left a dollar tip on a forty cent meal and went out.

Back in my room, I glanced again at the list. Wayne Watkins and Bill Agar. These were the two men I needed to know about in El Dorado. The first saloon I went to, I left after a short while. They really wasn't the talkative kind of folks in there. They seemed interested in only one thing, drinking. The next one was far better. Watkins still lived there in town. Agar had a small place just east of town now. He had recently stepped down as sheriff of El Dorado. Then I was told that the new sheriff was a man named Tom Evans.

49

Well how about that I thought. *Three rats in one trap.
It was enough for tonight* I thought and stood up to go.
That's when I saw them. A table at the back of the room.
There sat Buck Moore and four other men, one of which
wore a badge. I wanted to find out who they were, but
wasn't ready for trouble. *Not with Moore, not just yet*, so
I eased on out.

In my room I packed my few belongings for in the
morning and laid down on the bed. I'd slept very little
since this all began, but that night I did. Maybe it was
because I felt I was getting ready for what I had in my
mind. I had breakfast at the same diner the next morning
and saw that girl Lily again. She thanked me for the
generous tip last night and asked if I wanted coffee.

"Yes Ma'am," I said.

When she brought it back, she said, "you're up
early."

"Yes Ma'am," I said, "pulling out today. Got some
business in a place called Emporia."

"Mind if I ask what it is you do?"

"Looking for land for a group of investors back east.
I tried Wichita before coming here, but there was no land
available around there."

50

"I bet not, not unless you're willing to bow down to David Douglas anyway."

"He have a big place?" I asked.

"The biggest this side of Texas."

"Well if I have no luck in Emporia, I may just head to Texas myself," I told her.

"If so, you stop back through and see me, okay." she said smiling.

"You can count on it. The food's not that good, but the service is second to none."

I saw her no more after she brought my food. I left there and went to the livery. As I rode toward Emporia, my thoughts went in a hundred directions. One of which was that girl, Lily. "Damn fool," I muttered to myself. "Here you are about to start a war and you've got a girl on your mind."

My plans on how to deal with the men who had murdered my brothers was still working in my mind too. Douglas' fate was already decided. He would be the last one though. I wanted him to see all of the others that he had bought and used for his deal to go before him. To be always wondering, but never knowing when his number was up. In Emporia, I found that nothing much had changed.

William Parsons was still the judge and Percy Cain, the sheriff. I did find out that the sheriff had a new deputy, Abe Johnson. Well these boys were just making it easier and easier for me. It was to go back to the ranch and do some real planning now. I rode into El Dorado about five in the evening. Stabled my horse and went to the diner. After I was seated, an older man came to the table to take my order. "What'll it be?" he asked me.

"Well, to start with good sir, how about Miss Lily for my waitress?"

The old man looked at me and said, now don't you think if she was here, I wouldn't be out here."

"Her day off?" I asked.

"No sir, that pa of hers found out where she was and came and dragged her home again. That gal is over twenty years old and has a right to decide things for herself. David Douglas," he spat. "Just because he's richer than anybody around, he thinks his word is law. I hate the day that man ever came to this part of the country. Well, enough of that anyway."

51

"What sounds good to you today?" he asked.

I ordered my meal and met him at the counter to get me a cup and a pot of coffee. *Douglas, that girl's father? Well if I had no business starting anything with Lily before, I dang sure didn't now.* I decided not to stay the night in El Dorado after all, so when I finished eating, I went to the stable. While I saddled my horse, the livery man struck up a conversation.

"Terrible thing about that girl from the diner, don't you think?"

"Lily, you mean?" I answered.

"Yep," he said. "A man beating on a woman like that. That's wrong, just wrong."

"He beat her?" I asked, "his own daughter?"

"Step-daughter," said the old man. "Her ma was killed in a fall from a horse not too long after Douglas got the ranch started. She was a very nice lady. The girl Lily probably wasn't more than twelve when her ma died. Lots of folks around here didn't think it fitting that he kept her at the ranch after that. Him just being her step-father and all. A young couple here in town offered to adopt her, but Douglas would hear nothing of it."

"He beat her?" I asked again.

He nodded his head. "This ain't the first time either.

Every chance she gets, she'll take off and come here or Wichita. Then one day, he'll show and force her to go back home."

"Won't the law do anything?"

"Sure, they'll do something. As long as it's something Douglas told 'em to do."

"Well I wish her the best," I told the livery man as I mounted. I pitched him a dollar and rode out.

52

As I rode, I thought, *it's a shame a man like Douglas can only die once. But even that once would free that girl from him as well as pay for what he'd done to my brothers.*

No sooner was I in front of bunkhouse than Fence walked out. "Any problems?" I asked him.

"Not a thing out of Douglas, if that's what you mean," said Fence. "I'll take you horse Boss. You look plumb tuckered out."

Later over coffee, I told him all I'd found out and also about Lily.

"Boss, if it's none of my business just so say, but what is it exactly you're planning to do. What I mean is, are you just getting information to turn over to the territory marshal or something else?"

53

"Well Fence," I said, "you're a true friend and took up here with me and all. I reckon you've got a right to know. That way if you want no part of it, you can ride out. No hard feelings. I'm about to take a war to Douglas and all those others, the likes of which they can't imagine. My brothers were good men Fence. Never done no wrong to nobody. Unlike Douglas, we never planned to take over everything around here, we just wanted something better. Honest men stand no chance against men like Douglas though. So I aim to thin the herd a little. I have to tell you, at first, I planned to kidnap everyone involved with their death and take them out and hang them."

"And now?" asked Fence.

"Now, I intend to make them hang themselves. If you're with me I'll go into more detail."

"I ain't going nowhere," he said.

"Good," I told him, "I could really use your help. How long you been in these parts?"

"Born in Lawrence," he said. "Never been out of Kansas."

"Fence, how well do you know the area north east of El Dorado?" I asked him.

"Pretty good I'd say. I lived just outside of town for

about a year after I left Lawrence."

"Good," I said, "I need a well-hidden place to camp for a while without worrying about being seen by anybody."

"Got a place in mind already. Been a while since I was there though. Might need to ride up and take a gander. Make sure some folks ain't moved in on it."

54

"Make us up a pack for a few days and we'll head up there tomorrow," I told him.

Over supper, we talked more and I ask him what year he left Lawrence.

"I was off working cattle for a feller when Quantrill attacked 'em. Lost my ma and pa and a sister in that raid," he said.

"I'm sorry to hear that," I told him. "My company was sent out after them after that."

"You catch 'em?" he asked.

"A couple, but Quantrill and most of them disappeared like smoke after that raid. You can't kill what you can't even find."

"Soon as we heard what was going on me and all the boys on the ranch headed that way all out. We run into some of 'em. Had a little gun battle for a minute, but they jumped on their horses and ours was plumb tuckered out already. I did get a good look at a couple of 'em. It's faces I'll never forget."

The following morning, we rode out, headed for El Dorado. I thought about Lily on the way, though I tried not to. Not wanting to be seen just now, we rode wide of town and came back to the trail farther on.

Just before dark, Fence stopped and said, "this is it

Boss."

He left the trail and soon we were skirting around a good sized lake. It wasn't long before we came to a little cabin, half falling in.

"How did you ever find this place?"

"Didn't," said Fence, "I built it. Course it was a little better shape back then."

"This is perfect," I told him.

55

We spent the next two days cleaning and patching up the cabin and the little pole corral out behind it. The third morning, we rode out and back toward El Dorado.

Lack of good sense got the better of me and we rode into town and right to the diner. I at least wanted to find out if she was alright.

The old man saw me and came to our table. "Ain't seen you around in a while?"

"Been busy looking for land to build that ranch," I lied. "I wanted to see if you'd heard if Lily is okay."

"If you mean hurt, I'm sure she's fine. Once Douglas has her back on the ranch, he don't bother her. He just don't want her leaving or being around anybody that ain't on the ranch."

"Almost like he has something to hide."

"Yeah," said the old man, "just like that."

About then, I looked up to see Buck Moore come in the door.

When he saw me, he came straight to the table. "We don't need nor want your kind around here Rayburn."

"You do that deciding or your boss?" I ask.

I knew Moore for what he was, a gun-man. I, also, knew I wasn't one. While I'm a good shot if given time

I'm no gun-slick.

He mouthed off something about Henry, but I didn't take his bait. "Mind if we eat before we go?"

He saw I wasn't going for it so he snarled, "yeah eat your damn food, then ride out or I'll ride you out Friend."

"You bet," I told him and just then the old man came with our food.

Moore turned and walked out of the diner.

"What was that all about?" the old man asked me.

56

When I've got more time, I'll tell you. I heard that," I told Fence after he walked away.

"You got good ears," he said as he holstered his pistol. "I heard what that sheriff said," Fence told me. "I knew he was trying to goad you into something."

"I appreciate it Fence, but on a bad day, I'm smarter than Sheriff Buck Moore."

We rode back to the ranch without stopping in Wichita. Riding in a little after dark, I saw a faint light under the door of the barn and whispered to Fence.

We stopped our horses right there and climbed down. I pointed for him to go to one side of the barn and I went to the other. I peeked in through a crack in a shutter and after a minute I saw movement. A man stood up on the far side of the barn from me. I was about to open the shutter when he lowly called out to somebody else.

Another man stood up no more than three feet from me inside the barn.

"I thought I heard horses for a minute there," said the first to stand.

"I ain't heard nothing," said the one near me. "You're just jumpy Mike that's all."

"You damn right I am Jim," he answered back. "I don't like fooling with dynamite one bit."

Oh these boys was making it too easy. Dollars to doughnuts, this was Mike Smith and Jim Shumaker.

I slipped around the barn to where Fence was and motioned him to follow me. We went back and stood in the shadow of the bunkhouse.

57

Maybe ten minutes later, the barn door creaked open. They had doused the lamp or candle they'd been using, so it was totally dark now.

They took a few steps and one of them stopped to light a smoke. As the match flared, Fence and I stepped out and I said loudly, "don't even flinch boys."

"Who the hell is that!" shouted one of them.

"Well, who'd you come to see!" I shouted back at him.

The match dropped to the ground and as it did so, both me and Fence fired. We saw two stabs of flame as they fired, but one went into the dirt at his feet and the other went skyward.

"We're done," came a voice from the dark.

"Throw your guns toward the bunkhouse then," I told him.

I heard a thud as one hit the ground, but not the other.

"Throw the other one too or we'll open up again," I told him.

After a good minute, I heard the other one hit.

"Now walk over here," I said. I whispered for Fence to get a lamp from inside, "but don't light it yet."

As he came out the door, I could make out one figure

coming toward us.

"Where's your friend?" I asked

"Dead," he replied. "That's why it took me a minute to throw his gun. I had to find it first."

I told Fence to light the lamp.

"I need a doctor Mister I'm hit bad."

As the lamp came to life, I could see he wasn't lying.

"Gut shot," I said. "If a doctor was here right now, he couldn't help you I told him."

58

I told Fence to check the other one. The gut shot man staggered and sat down hard on the ground.

"What's your name?" I asked him.

He stammered out, "Smith, Mike Smith."

Fence walked back and shook his head. "He's dead alright. Caught it in the head."

"I guess Shumaker is the lucky one," I told him. "He died quick. I've seen it take hours with a gut shot."

"You gotta help me," he said. "Shoot me again at least."

"You're not worth a second shot," I told him. "Where's that dynamite planted?"

He made as if to deny it, but I told him we'd been right outside and heard them talking.

"Base of the roof poles," he said and then said no more.

"How about some coffee Fence?"

"Yes sir, that sounds good," said Fence.

We walked inside and I started a fire enough to boil coffee.

"Which one you think you got?" he asked

"Well you're taller, so you probably got the one in the

head," I told him.

Later laying in my bunk, I took out the list of names given to me by Sheriff Banks. That was two I could scratch from my list. Parsons and Cain I'd written 'later' beside their names. I'd been told they pulled out for California.

The next morning, we hauled the two bodies to the back edge of the ranch and in a spot where we couldn't be seen from the Douglas' range, we buried them.

Back at the ranch, I went in the barn and found that dynamite. Two sticks on either side had been tied to the support post. A fuse run up the post and into a lamp hanging on each.

"If we'd came in here at dark and lit those lamps, we would, also, have lit the fuses," I told him.

59

That finished, we took the wagon and headed to Dodge city. We got what goods we needed and back out of town without being seen by Sheriff Banks. I liked the man, but right now, I didn't need him asking too many questions about my plans. In fact, the fewer people that knew about it the better.

Right now even Fence didn't know everything.

60

CHAPTER THREE

Vengeance

At the ranch we got everything ready to take the supplies and the horses Fence had bought for me to the camp above El Dorado. This trip, I planned to bypass Wichita and El Dorado altogether. Hopefully without being seen by anyone.

While I'd bought supplies in Dodge, I'd sent Fence to hire the two men who'd stayed at the ranch with him before to come back. I also left my old horse Gus in the stable. Should somebody get nosy, it would appear that I was there if my horse was.

The one I rode now was mouse colored. From a distance you'd think it was Gus, but she was far younger.

As I hoped, we reached Fence's old cabin without seeing a soul. Then I set about looking over where we was. I was hoping to find a place to hold some men for a while without having to build anything. If I wasn't going to hang them, I had to have some place to keep them until they signed a statement as to their part in my brothers' murders.

It took me two days of walking over the area, but I found it. A creek had at some point fed that big lake, but was long dry now. The banks were eight to ten feet high in places. The morning after I found the dry creek, me and Fence started cutting trees.

61

They weren't as big as what you'd used for a cabin. Didn't need to be.

I aimed to build up two walls of them about ten feet apart in that creek bed. When I was satisfied that the walls were strong enough, we began laying a floor of logs over them. Running bank to bank with a couple of feet extra on either side. In one corner, I left a four foot by four foot opening for putting in and taking out prisoners.

Fence took all of this in without ever asking what it was for, until the day it was finished.

That evening as we ate supper, he looked at me and said Boss, just what is it that pit's for?"

"Bad men," I told him.

"You mean them fellers who hanged your brothers don't you?"

"That's exactly who I mean Fence. I intend to put all but one of them in that pit."

"Why not all?"

"Because I intend to kill Douglas outright," I told him.

"So you're not gonna kill these others?"

I shook my head, "not if they'll do what I ask of

them. Oh I intend for them to endure some hardship. Staying in that cramped pit for a while and having only enough food and water to live. When I have them all, I'll let them plead guilty of what they've done and go free. Leastways until the law catches up to them. After doing some talking and writing out some papers, I'll let the ones in the pit go free."

"Ain't they just as much to blame?" he asked me.

"They are," I said, "but left of their own selves, they never would have done it. Douglas, with his power and money is what caused it."

62

After supper, I took my old Union uniform out that I had brought from the ranch. Taking out my knife, I cut off every brass button, stripe and a medal I'd been given from it.

The taking of these men I would do at night.

Thus, the dark clothes and I'd ride that black horse I bought. My hair and beard had grown rather long by now and I didn't think anybody could recognize me if I was seen. The next day in my regular clothes I rode into El Dorado alone. I guess I was testing to see if anyone knew me and, also, to ask about Lily. I couldn't seem to get that girl out of my head.

I didn't go to the diner. If anybody here would know me, it'd be that old cook there. Instead, I went to the saloon. I saw no sign of him, but I learned that Tom Evans had become the new sheriff of El Dorado.

I was, also, told by a man after I bought him a drink that Sam Wilde had been made sheriff in Emporia and in turn made Abe Johnson, his deputy.

That same man told me that the old sheriff and their judge hadn't just rode away to California as was thought either. The bodies of both men had been found in a ditch, shot in the head and covered with brush.

How about that I thought. *They must have got*

crossways with Douglas someway, Maybe demanded more money or something. So Douglas killed 'em or had it done. I didn't care either way it just made my life easier.

I asked several people if that pretty little waitress was back at the diner, but they all said no.

I rode to camp pleased with what I'd found out, except that Lily had not gotten away again.

The next day I sat in Fence's cabin and pulled my list from my pocket.

63

With my new knowledge, I checked off the names. In Emporia, Judge Parsons and Sheriff Cain were dead. I scratched their names off.

Fence and I had took care of Mike Smith and Jim Shumaker, back at the ranch that night.

I now had two men in Emporia to take. Sam Wilde and Abe Johnson. The new sheriff and deputy.

In El Dorado I had three men. Judge Watkins, Bill Agar, the old sheriff and Tom Evans, the new one.

In Wichita, I had three as well. Judge Avery, John Sikes the old sheriff and my old 'friend' Buck Moore.

I made up my mind to start in Emporia and I would leave headed there tomorrow.

Fence wanted to go something awful, but I told him to hold on. That if all went well there, I'd need him more in Wichita and El Dorado.

He didn't like it, but he agreed. Two nights later after midnight I pounded on the door of the sheriffs pretending to be drunk. After a few minutes, the opened and there stood Wilde and Johnson. I staggered around, fussing that the bar keep wouldn't give me another drink.

"Say you got a drink in there?" I asked.

64

"Sure we have," said the sheriff, "come on in."

I knew their plan was to get me inside, then throw me in jail. I had my pistol stuck down the back of my britches. Once inside, they stopped to lock door behind us and when they turned around, they came face to face with my pistol. Neither of them was armed. Why should they be, they were in the office.

I pulled two short lengths of rope from my pocket. I made Wilde tie Johnson's hands behind his back, then I tied Wilde's.

"I don't know who you are Mister, but you're making a bad mistake doing this."

"No you boys made the mistake when you arrested my brothers for no reason, beat my youngest brother half to death and then you boys, along with Parsons and Cain hanged them."

At this they both squirmed and pulled against their ropes. They knew now who they were dealing with.

"Careful," I said, "you'll get loose. If that happens, I'm just going to shoot you both in the head right here."

I took a quick look out the window and saw nobody moving. With my pistol and one of theirs, I opened the door and pushed them out.

"Open your mouth to holler or try to run and I'll kill

you without blinking," I said. I turned them down the first alleyway. Their horses and mine was tied there.

Two nights later without a bite to eat and little water, I untied their hands one at a time and pushed them through that four by four trap door. I moved the lock in place and went to the cabin.

I spoke loudly enough to wake Fence before reaching the door, but there was no need.

He stood in the shadows against the wall. "Glad you're back Boss," he said. "I was beginning to worry."

"Two wolves in the trap," I told him as we went in.

"Kept supper warm just in case," said Fence.

"I could eat," I told him.

While I ate, he asked a million questions. How I'd got the drop on 'em and such.

I told him all of it.

65

"That's it?" he said when I finished.

"That's it," I told him.

"They don't sound smart enough to be no sheriff or deputy." he said.

"They're not," I told him. "They're just holding the jobs that Douglas put them in. In case he needed something done that had to look legal. Before I brought these in, he had his men in the three closest towns. Men in his employ, that would do whatever he said. I'd say that gives him leeway in doing just about whatever he wants in a big area and nobody to say no, wouldn't you? Well I just shorted him two of those," I told Fence.

"When are you going after the next ones?" he asked.

"Two days," I told him. "Wichita is where he buys his supplies for the ranch and does most of his business. If I hit it next, he may catch on that something's happening before I get El Dorado. So, El Dorado it is," I told him. "I've got three men to get there, Fence. Judge Watkins, The old sheriff, Bill Agar and the new one Tom Evans."

66

If you're still game for it, I could use your help on this," I said. "I think I can take all three pretty easy, but running herd on all three to get them back here I'm not so sure about."

"I'm with you Boss, you know that."

"Good," I said, "besides the help I'll have good company."

Two evenings later, the two of us were hid out in a clump of trees near a little farm outside of town. A little before dark, I eased my way on foot up to the barn and went in. I'd grown up on a farm and knew that just at dark we always brought in the mules and whatever tool we'd been using that day to the barn. I was hoping Agar did the same. If not, I'd have to give him time to get settled down and go in the cabin after him. Knowing he used to be a sheriff and not just one of Douglas' posers I'd have to go careful. I was sure he could shoot.

Ten minutes after I was in the barn, I heard the big doors open. Then he led a mule and wagon loaded with tools in. He stripped the mule of her harness and pitched some hay into her stall, then came back to the wagon. I think at first, he was going to leave the tools where they were for the night. Then he changed his mind and began putting them in their place. I had noticed he wore no side arm. When he came back to the wagon for more tools, I stood there with my pistol aimed at the middle of his chest.

I saw the recognition and fear flash in his eyes.

"Two choices," I said, "die right here or come with me peacefully."

He started babbling that he only did what Douglas forced him to.

"I know that," I told him, "but it don't much matter. You still done it and my brothers never robbed or hurt anybody."

I grabbed one of his arms and forced it behind him, then took the other am. With his hands tied behind him, I sat him down hard on the ground and went and got his mule. I put her back in harness, draged him up into the wagon and sat him down again.

67

Before we reached town; I had Fence gag him and lay him down. Next, I had Fence take the wagon around back of the and wait. I eased my way down the side of the house and sure enough I found a window partly opened. Quietly, I climbed in it and made my way through the small house. Just then I heard noises. Kitchen noises, he was fixing his supper.

I walked over and stood beside the doorway leading into the kitchen. Shortly, he came through the door and headed for a chair to sit down. He set his food on a small table and sat down. When he looked up, I stood not three feet from him with my pistol pointed at him.

"Here what's this?" he said. "I keep no money here in the house."

"I'm not here to rob you," I told him.

"To kill me. Why I've made no threats to Douglas, like them fools, Parsons and Cain."

"No, maybe not, but you did his dirty work in hanging my brother for him."

68

Now I saw that same fear on his face that Agar had. "Get up," I told him.

"Look you don't have to kill me," he said. "I'll go to the bank tomorrow and give you every penny Douglas paid me and whatever I have above that."

"The greed of Douglas and twelve of you others caused the senseless death of my four brothers. Do you think any amount of money could make up for that? Money got you into this mess, but it won't get you out," I told him.

With his hands behind him and gagged, I pulled him around behind the house and put him in the wagon. When he saw Agar already there a new batch of fear hit him.

"One more," I told Fence and we rode away.

On the way I asked Fence if he'd ever had a run in with this Evans.

"None that I know of," he said.

"I have a plan then," I told him.

I, also, realized that the wagon we rode was my own. The walls and roof we'd put on to make it our chuck wagon had been removed, but I was sure it was the same wagon.

Fence pulled the wagon into the alley between the

sheriff's office and the general store.

"Okay," I told him, "now, do as we planned and don't let him give you no for an answer."

Agar and Watkins was bound, gagged and their upper half was covered by a piece of sacking I'd found under the wagon seat. I heard them coming and blended back into the shadows against the wall.

"Two of 'em," Fence was saying. "Just laying in the road on the way into town."

Evans leaned over the wagon and lit a match.

69

As the match flamed to life, I put his lights out with the butt of my pistol. Together, we tied his hands and put him in the wagon bed. It was breaking dawn as we drove up beside the pit. Wilde and Johnson made no noise in the pit and I figured they were sleeping. I roused Agar and Watkins and pulled them from the wagon.

Opening the pit door, I forced first Agar down a rope. Then the judge, against protest. I think he fell the last few feet. Evans was still out cold. I guess I'd hit him a little harder than I thought. I pulled the rope up out of the pit and made a loop in the end. I put it over his head and under his arms and between Fence and myself, we lowered him down. I called down for Agar to untie it.

"When are you gonna tell us what this is all about!" he shouted up.

"When I'm ready," I told him. "In the meantime, if you want anything to eat or drink, don't cause me no trouble."

With that, I shut the trap door and locked it.

Fence and I had been up for twenty four straight hours. We went to the cabin to remedy that. I woke up around two that evening to the smell of cooking. Fence had done been to the pit and lowered down a bucket of water. "That sheriff's awake," he said, "and cussing like a sailor."

"Good," I said, "I was beginning to think I'd whacked him too hard."

"It's hot out there Boss," he said "They got to be in pure misery."

70

"Good," I said, "I have been ever since they hanged my brothers. You're not going soft on me are you Fence?"

"No sir," he said, "just remind me now and then not to make you mad at me."

After we finished, he fixed up a bucket of food and took to the prisoners. When he was back, he asked me what next.

"I figure in the morning, we'll head to Wichita," I told him. "I have three more there for the pit. It'll surprise me if I can get all three of them here alive though. That new sheriff, Buck Moore and me have butted heads a couple of times already. I may have to kill him."

"If you do go cautious," said Fence. "I've heard of him. He's a gun hand and a fast one I've heard. He's killed at least four men over in Dodge City," said Fence.

"I've killed quite a few men myself," I told him.

"Yes sir, but you had a reason. They was a war going on and you was a soldier. He killed them men for no good reason at all."

In Wichita, Avery and Sikes was no problem at all to take, but Moore was nowhere to be found. If he was in Wichita, he was hiding and I just didn't believe that.

When I was afraid to wait longer and these two found missing, we headed for the cabin.

"I'll just have to come back for him," I told Fence.

At supper that next evening I asked Fence if he'd ever cut hair.

"Just my own," he said. Jokingly.

Looking at him, I said, "well you've still got both of your ears, so let's have a go at it."

71

I shaved first, while he honed his knife and razor. Considering the situation, I thought he did a first class job.

Early the next morning, I dressed in my usual clothes.

"No more hiding out?" he asked me.

"Wouldn't help," I said. "One word and he'd know who I was anyway."

Before leaving I went to the pit.

One at a time, I had Fence them up from the hole. I'd stayed up most of the night writing out a letter admitting to their part in the murder of my brothers for payment from David Douglas. In turn, I made each of them read and then sign it, telling them it was that or a bullet. I put it in an envelope and wrote Sheriff Bank's name on it. Before I left, I went behind the cabin and searched the wagon. Sure enough, under a loose board under the seat, I found just over seventy four hundred dollars wrapped in a bandana.

Then I talked to Fence and gave two envelopes to him. "Fence, wait two days after I'm gone, then I want you to get your things ready. Go by and drop a rope down the hatch door and ride for Dodge City," I told him.

"What about you?" he asked.

"I've still got two men to get," I told him. "Open the

hatch tell them they're free and ride out. Don't hang around and give them a chance to jump you. It'll take them a while to walk out of here back to El Dorado."

We'd let Agar's mule go as soon as we'd got back to the cabin.

Now I had busted a wheel on the wagon as well.

Are you coming back to the ranch?" he asked me.

"If I can, I'll see you at the ranch in a few days," I said. "If not and Douglas gets taken down by the territorial Marshal, the ranch is yours. That's what the letter in that second envelope says."

I shook his hand and rode out."

72

That night I camped just outside of Wichita. Sitting beside the fire that night, I thought about the boys. Especially Matt. He'd been nothing but a kid when I left for the war and now only a short time spent with him after we came home.

As much as I enjoyed that first drive with all of us. I'd give up that memory to have them back. Just at that moment, something hit my fire and threw hot embers all over me. I fell over backward and as I hit the ground; I heard the report of the rifle. I rolled into the darkness as quick as possible. Crawling flat on the ground, I managed to get myself behind a good sized rock between me and the direction that bullet had come from. For the sound of that shot to take that long to reach me, the shooter was some distance away. I believe if it had been day-light, I'd be a goner right now. Mighty close as it was.

Just then, it sounded like a half a dozen rifles opened up on my camp. The only way for me to get to my horse would be toward the gunfire. I crawled another thirty or forty feet and when I stood up, I did some running. I held that pace until I could run no more and fell to the ground.

73

I hid most of the day in a stand of trees. Then in the evening, I lit out walking at a fast pace. I hoped the direction I traveled would carry me to the back side of my ranch. The place where I'd found the creek dammed. It might slow up my pursuers too, thinking they had their rabbit running right for the snare, Douglas' ranch. If not, I stood little chance of making it to mine. Even running, I would never outrun them on horses.

About mid-day, I was climbing over a high, steep hill. There off in the distance, I saw what I knew had to be that huge ranch house of Douglas'. *I might just make it after all* I thought and picked up my pace.

By dark I was worn out and stopped. I was now only a short distance from where I had tore down that dam.

I started to go on to the ranch, but didn't know what may be waiting for me in the dark. I had to move slow until I knew if Fence was there or some of Douglas' men.

Maybe Fence hadn't bothered to come back to the ranch at all or had and when I didn't show up after a few days like I'd said, he rode out again. The night was pitch black. If there was a moon, it stayed well hidden behind high clouds. Being so dark made it impossible for me to have even a small fire. The light from it could and might be seen for many miles on a night like this and I knew my pursuers were close.

If I stood and looked east, I could see the lights from the Douglas Ranch.

74

The light of a fire along with the smell of wood smoke would surely draw them right to me. I knew at least four men, maybe more still trailed me at this very minute. What I didn't know was if they were lawmen or gun hands hired by Douglas. Either one would mean the end of me and the end of justice for my brothers. So I sat in a hollow place in a steep hillside above the creek. Sat because it wasn't big enough to stretch out my six foot frame in any direction. For now, I would sit here in the dark and hope no one found me, then again, I hoped they did. *How did it all come to this* I wondered *but I knew the answer to that question all too well. Greed.*

75

CHAPTER FOUR

Justice and Love

Before daylight though, I was up and moving again toward the ranch house and what was possibly my own death. Sitting there last night, I'd felt that my vengeance had turned into something else now. Hate and I had hoped it would not. For I knew what hatred could turn me into. Someone that could kill my enemies without remorse. My time in the war had proven that to me. I thought of that and then I thought about a pretty girl in a diner, what now seemed like a hundred years ago. A girl that while I couldn't say I loved her, I'd very much like to see if it could come to that. Not if I let this hatred take over though. If so, I'd go straight to Douglas' big fancy ranch house and kill any man who stood between me and him. Then I'd shoot Douglas over and over until I knew there was no hope that anyone could save him.

She'd never want anything to do with me then, even though he treated her badly. Still it had to be settled one way or another.

I couldn't live with myself if I just rode away and let Douglas get away with the senseless murder of my brothers.

76

I eased my way up to the back of the barn. A light smoke went up from the chimney. *Bad guys eat too* I thought. In the corral, I saw Gus standing three legged waiting for his morning feeding.

Two minutes later and the bunkhouse door opened and Fence stepped out. As he got near, I spoke only loud enough for him to hear. "You alone Fence?" I asked him.

"That you Boss?" he asked.

"Yeah it's me," I told him, "or what's left of me. I've had a peck of trouble."

"I thought you was dead for sure," said Fence. "That black horse wondered in here two days ago."

"You had any trouble here?" I asked.

"Not a peep," he said.

He fed Gus and I walked back to the bunkhouse with him. When we went in, he said, "I've got coffee on and I'll fix you something to eat Boss."

I sat down at the table and begin telling all that had happened since we separated at his old cabin. When I finished, he said he'd taken that letter to Sheriff Banks and was told he was sending for a U.S. Marshal.

He asked how you got them folks to sign, but all I said was, "nobody got killed. You still ain't got Buck

Moore then?" he asked.

"Never even got a chance to try," I told him. "Moore must have found them people gone and went to Douglas, probably before we even let them go. Otherwise, they wouldn't have been on me so quick unless they was already out looking."

"What do we do now?" he asked.

"I don't really know," I told him. "If we can hold out long enough maybe that marshal can get here and help us out."

77

"What have we got in the way of arms here?" I asked Fence.

"Four rifles, six pistols and them four sticks of dynamite we took from them fellers," said Fence.

"Shells?" I asked.

"Maybe a hundred rounds for the rifles and half that for the pistols," he said.

"There was at least four men and I believe more trailing me out there. One of them boys can shoot too. That one shot into my fire that night was from a ways off and if his shot had been two foot higher, we wouldn't be setting here talking," I told Fence.

Just then, we both heard the sound of a horse coming in the yard. I went to the window and peeked out through a crack in the shutter.

I knew what my eyes told me, but I couldn't believe it. Lily. She climbed down and started for the door. At the window, I spoke softly to her. "Are you alone?" I asked her.

"Yes," she said. "Is that you?"

"Come on to the door" I opened it quickly and she darted in.

She came to me and hugging me said, "I thought they

had killed you."

"They tried," I told her, "they tried."

"Boss I'm going out to feed the horses," said Fence

"Would you put hers in the barn too?" I asked him.

"Sure thing Boss," he said.

"What are you doing here?" I ask her.

"I only learned last night that Dan Rayburn and Kent Waters was the same person." she said.

"How much do you know about what's going on?" I asked her. "Not much," she said. "I'd overhear a little here and there is all."

I got up and poured her a cup of coffee and sat back down. "Who knows you're here?"

"Nobody. They all went to Wichita this morning and I used it as a chance to escape.

78

Over the next two hours, I explained everything that had happened.

"Dan, you've got to leave here. David has people everywhere doing his dirty work. They mean to kill you." she said.

"I mean to do the same to them Lily," I told her.

"But there's so many of them and you're all alone."

"I've got Fence," I told her.

"I've never met anybody like you," she said. I liked you from the first time we met at the diner. Why did you tell me your name was Kent?" she asked.

"I was there trying to get some information and didn't want anybody to know who I was. I didn't know until I came back through town and to the diner that Douglas was your step-father and that he had come and forced you to go back to the ranch."

"Step-father. He's my jailer is what he is."

She went on to tell me how her real father had died in the war. Mother couldn't stand it there without him, so she sold the plantation and her business and brought us west for a new start. She started the ranch and David was one of the men she hired to help build the house. By the time it was finished, she had fallen in love with him. I guess him being from the south himself and having been a soldier. Maybe it reminded her of my father. I don't know."

79

"Wait," I said, "that ranch was started by your mother?"

She shook her head yes.

"I've been told he had money backers in England," I told her.

"That's the story he wants everybody to believe," she said. "That's the main reason he doesn't want me off the ranch. He's afraid I'll tell the truth about everything. He was okay at first. Right after they married, but as time went on, he turned mean toward me and my mother. One night I heard them arguing over the way he was spending so much money and the kind of men he was hiring to work at the ranch. The following day she was going to ride into town alone. She told me she needed to see a judge and her banker. When she wasn't back by dark, David and some of his men went looking for her. They found her about three miles outside of town. She'd been thrown from her horse and hit her head on a rock, he told me."

I made her stay there that night.

Fence and I slept in the barn so she could have her privacy.

In the middle of the night, I saddled her horse, led it out front and gave it a slap on the rear. Things may be looking up some for me, so I didn't need Douglas to start hollering I was a horse thief. I knew it would go home and I knew the ranch would be the first place he looked for her. It didn't matter, let him come. It was time this was over one way or another.

Just before daylight we heard horses coming.

80

Looking at Fence, I said, "this it old buddy. This is your last chance to jump from this burning wagon before it goes over the cliff."

"I bet that gal's got coffee on," he said and picked up his rifle.

Together we walked out the door of the barn figuring to be cut down at any minute. Eight men on horseback sat there. It wasn't the men I was expecting though. The three in front was Sheriff Banks from Dodge City. Beside him was Sheriff Matthews from Kansas City. The third man I didn't know, but I could see that U.S. Marshal badge shining on his chest. The other five turned out to be Mr. Gregory that Fence had worked for and four of his riders.

"You Rayburn?" the marshal asked me.

"Yes sir," I told him.

"We need to talk Son," he said.

Lily had opened the door by now and she said, "I have coffee on.

As Fence passed me, he said, "I told she did. She just seemed like that kind of girl to me. "

After everybody who wanted it got coffee, they went out. All but me, Lily, the sheriff's and the marshal.

"Mr. Rayburn," said the marshal.

"Please call me Dan," I told him.

"Okay Dan. I got a wire from Sheriff Matthews about what was going on. I was trying to clear my slate to come here when I got another wire from Sheriff Banks. I had both of them meet me in El Dorado. They filled me in on all they knew about what was going on and Sheriff Banks gave me this he said, holding up the paper I'd made them all sign.

81

"I don't know how you got them to sign it and maybe it's best if I don't, but it's one smart move on your part. Both of these sheriffs seem to think a lot of you, so it would have been a shame to hunt you down, if you'd just started going out and killing these folks with no proof of why. I've already arrested Judge Watkins, Bill Agar and Tom Evans before we left El Dorado. They now sit in their own jail.

In Wichita, Sheriff Banks ran into his friend, Mr. Gregory and some his boys who helped us round up Judge Avery, John Sikes and tried to find Sheriff Buck Moore, but was unable to do so. Avery and Sikes are in jail too. I've also wired another U.S. Marshal to go to Emporia and arrest Sam Wilde and Abe Johnson. Those are the seven signatures on this list."

"You'll find Buck Moore at the Double 'D' ranch," said Lily.

"No Ma'am, we won't," said the marshal. "When we didn't find Moore in town, we rode out there. Not a soul to be found," he said.

"They've got word you're on to them and they're running," said Dan.

"They won't get far," the marshal said. "The name Buck Moore struck me, so I checked into him. There's already wanted posters out on him for the death of at least a half dozen men. Some in fair fights, some out and out murder. As for David Douglas, I was hoping one of you could give us a description, so can get flyers out on him as well."

"May I go to the ranch?" Lily asked him. "I'd like to take a bath and change," she said.

"I'll ask Sheriff banks to ride over with you," the marshal told her.

"I'll go," said Dan.

"I don't think that would be wise," said the marshal. "Should either of them show up, it might turn into gun play. This young lady could get hurt. I'm sure the sheriff will be glad to. I'll go ask him while you get ready Miss."

82

After he went out, I said, you'll have to take one of my horses."

"What about my horse?" she asked.

I turned him loose last night. I didn't know we were going to wake up to a yard full of lawmen this morning, but I didn't want Douglas yelling I'd stolen a horse from him."

"But I'm here," said Lily.

"Not that he would ever have known until both Fence and I were dead," Dan told her. "He's hurt you for the last time."

"You don't mind my staying here?" she asked.

"I'm glad you are," said Dan.

After they left, Dan asked the marshal who would be the judge for the men he had caught.

"A territorial judge is all I know," he told Dan. "I'm not sure which one."

"Thank you," said Dan.

Just before dark, Sheriff Banks and Lily came back.

"Thank you," I told the sheriff.

"You're welcome Dan," he told me. "You think you'll have any trouble the rest of the night?"

"We'll be fine," I told him. "Me and fence will take turns keeping watch."

"Well alright," he said. "I guess we'll head back to Dodge then."

"The marshal said he was going that way a little earlier," I told him.

83

"I have a feeling Douglas and Moore are miles from here by now," he said. "They knew their days were numbered around here.'"

"You're probably right," I told him, although I didn't believe it for a minute. Douglas was way too greedy to just ride away from all this. He was still close. Hid out somewhere, but close enough to keep up with what was going on.

Fence had cooked earlier and Lily had gone in to eat while I saw the sheriff off.

I tapped on the door and went in. "Oh it's you Dan. Why are you knocking on your own door?"

"I wasn't sure if you were still awake," I told her. "I thought I'd have another cup of coffee." I poured me a cup and sat down.

"Listen, if you're ready to go to bed, I can drink this in the barn," I told her."

"Don't be silly," she said. "Sit there and drink your coffee. Dan. I want to thank you so much for letting me stay here. I couldn't imagine being in that huge house and not even knowing for sure if David may come back or not."

"I glad to have you," I told her. "Lily," I said. "I thought about you a lot after the first time we met. Then when I found out that Douglas was your step-father, I told myself, knowing what I had to do it'd be best just to forget about you."

"Please don't," she said. "I thought about you too after he dragged me back to the ranch. You were so kind to me and such a gentleman. Then I kept hearing about a guy named Dan Rayburn and his brothers. How they had gotten rid of them, but you were still in their way. Then Buck told David you'd been sneaking around town, but calling yourself Kent Waters."

84

"Later, I found out that Dan was your real name and that you lived right here, not three miles away all the time. One day a man I didn't know came to the house and I listened as he told David about people going missing from Emporia, El Dorado and Wichita. David flew into a rage then. He sent for Buck and told him to put together some men and find you and kill you no matter what."

"They almost did too," I told her.

"Buck would come in every day and tell David how it was going. That's when I learned you were headed to your ranch. I started watching for every chance to get away to come and warn you. Then Buck came in and told him those people were back and that you had held them captive and made them sign something. He also told David they had lost your trail and that he'd had enough. He was riding out. Any other man, David would have killed, but I think he knew he was no match for Buck. When I woke up yesterday morning, I found myself alone. Not a soul was on the ranch, but me. That's when I saddled my horse and rode over here."

"I'm glad you did," I told her.

"Dan why is this land so important to David? Have you found gold or something?"

"No. It's just his greed Lily, wanting everything.

85

"Even then, it wouldn't be enough. He'll keep on taking and taking until someone stops him."

"Kill him you mean?" said Lily.

Dan told her then that it had first been his plan to kill every one of them involved. I"nstead, I held them captive a few days until they would sign that paper saying they were guilty and let them go. There are only two left that haven't faced their punishment yet. Buck Moore and David Douglas. By their own choice the only way to make them pay is to kill them. I intend to do just that. I hope killing Douglas won't cause bad feelings between us, but it's something I have to do."

"It won't change my feeling for you Dan. It's not like he ever tried to be a father to me or anything. I have always believed he never loved my mother. He only married her for her money and I think he had something to do with her death. When will you be going out looking for them?" she asked.

The sooner the better," said Dan, "but I have to know you're safe first. I'd like to take you to Dodge City and get you a room while me and Fence are gone."

"When?" she asked.

"How about tomorrow?" said Dan.

"I'd like to go home and get some things first," said

Lily.

"We'll go first thing in the morning," he told her.

Dan stood up and said, "well I guess I'll say goodnight then."

Lily stood too and kissed him on the cheek. "Goodnight Dan, and thank you for being who you are.

Fence was asleep when he went in the barn.

86

"I'll tell him in the morning what's going on and he can get things ready while I ride with Lily.

They went in that big house and he followed her up the staircase and to her room. She quickly packed a bag of her things and they went back downstairs. Lily turned and went to the office where he had first met David Douglas. She went to a large safe and opened it. Reaching in, she retrieved a large envelope. "This," she told him turning, "was left to me by my mother. Although, as soon as the man who brought it out from town left, David took it from me. It has been locked in here ever since. I was never allowed to open it."

"You ready??" Dan asked her.

"Fence will be waiting on us?" said Lily.

He sat his horse where the road to the ranch came into the main road. The three of them rode west to Dodge.

On the way, Dan told Lily, "I'm afraid the hotel in Dodge is not as nice as what you're used to."

"It'll be fine," she said. After a minute, she said, "I'm not some little princess Dan. My mother was born and raised poor. My father met her when they were just children. His father is the one who owned the plantation. He died when father was a young man and he inherited.

Then he asked Mother to marry him.

After my father was killed in the first year of the war, my mother gave every slave there their freedom. For the rest of the war we worked a garden enough to feed us.

87

"She taught me how to ride, how to shoot and how to grow a garden. Just before the war ended is when she sold the plantation. A twenty room house on fifteen hundred acres of land that neither of us cared for. I was twelve when we came west."

"I thought the house here was big," Dan told her.

"That was David's idea. He convinced Mother, to be a successful rancher, she needed that big house. The two of us would have been fine in a three room cabin."

When Lily was checked in at the hotel and Dan had dropped by to tell Sheriff Banks, she was there he and Fence rode out.

For the next six days, they crisscrossed and combed the whole area without a sign of Douglas or Moore.

Then they found themselves on the land, north of his and Douglas' ranch. The same route he'd traveled when running from Douglas' men.

Fence was the one to find the first sign. A horse's shoe had scratched a rock close to the creek. "Fresh too," Fence told him.

I had warned Fence earlier about the holes just right to break the leg of a man or horse. We decided to tie our horses and do some walking. If we were to find them, it would be easier to come up on them afoot anyway.

"Another sign. Hoof print this time.

Another hundred yards or so and we found the horse. Sure enough, he had stepped in a hole and broke a foreleg.

"Well at least they're human enough; they put the horse out of misery," I told Fence.

88

"Another hour it'll be dark," said Fence. "If we're getting out of here for now, we best be doing it. I'd like to keep this ole nag of mine," he said.

"You're right," I told him." Let's backtrack out of here far enough, so we can have a fire for coffee."

After we got our horses, we moved on another two miles or so on foot. We stopped and while I watered the horses at the creek and staked them out, Fence put coffee on to boil.

No sooner was the coffee done than I put out the fire. I explained to Fence that maybe they'd be wanting coffee too and build a fire. "If we got one going, we'd never see theirs."

I took a piece of jerked beef out of my saddlebag and stood chewing it and studying to area all around us. Just as I moved my head, I saw a flicker. I found the spot again and motioned for Fence to come there.

I pointed out where I wanted him to look and then he shook his head.

"I know right where they're at," I told Fence. "That last night I was out here. I sat in a hollow spot in a hillside. I'd bet money that's where they are."

"How far?" he asked me.

"About a mile past where we stopped earlier," I told

him.

"We gonna try it tonight?" he asked.

"One or both of would break a leg in the dark," I told him. "I'd say neither of them are early risers though."

It was light enough to see only a few feet in front of us when we left our camp the next morning. It was a slow go to start and I was nervous with anticipation too.

89

It wasn't long though when Fence whispered, "I smell smoke."

We split up and went toward the camp from opposite directions. From where I was, I could see only one person still rolled up in his blanket. I closed in a little more. It was just one man. I saw no horse tied up close by. *That must have been his horse back there* I thought.

Whoever it was, they were covered up head and ears. Maybe it was neither of the men we were looking for. I looked across the camp and motioned for Fence to hold still for a minute. I eased on closer until I was no more than five feet from the sleeping man.

"Time to rise and shine!" I shouted very loudly.

He came out of that blanket like it was on fire, pistol in hand.

"Drop that gun or die," I told Buck Moore.

"You go to hell Friend, he said.

I saw his hand twitch to bring his pistol up and let go on him. Mine had been aimed right at him all the time. He was hit in the chest, but still trying to raise his pistol.

"It's over Moore," I told him. "Drop your gun."

He had no choice in it. Suddenly, his legs sagged and he went to the ground, his pistol falling from his hand. I walked over and stood above him.

"Looking up," he said, "you," and then he fell face first to the rocky soil.

"Damn it," I swore as fence walked up.

"You got him Boss," he said. "You killed Buck Moore."

"Yeah," I said, "now I can't ask him where Douglas is."

"Douglas is right here Boy," said a voice behind me. "Why couldn't you just die like them brothers of yours?" he said.

90

I was about to turn and face him when I heard the shot. For a long second; I thought he'd shot me in the back. It would be just like him. Then I realized I wasn't hit and spun around on him only he wasn't standing there, but was laying on the ground.

Fence walked up beside me. "Sorry Boss, I know you really wanted to kill him yourself for what he did to your brothers, but then I saw his face and just fired without thinking."

"Thanks Fence," I said.

"I couldn't help it Dan. When he moved out of the shadows, I saw his face and knew that he was one of Quantrill's men that got away that day. Older, but it's him for sure."

"It's over then, for both of us Fence. Justice for your folks and my brothers has been served at last."

We found Douglas' horse tied a short distance away. Leading her back, we put both bodies over the saddle and tied them on.

That evening we rode into Dodge with them trailing behind and went straight to the sheriff's office.

I opened the door and said, "Sheriff Banks. we got something out here for you."

He stood up from the desk and followed me out.

Beside the horse he lifted Moore's head and said, "Buck Moore. There's a reward on this one." Then he raised the one of the smaller man, and looked at me. "Douglas?" he asked.

I shook my head yes.

"I've got no reward flyer on him," he said. He sent a passing boy for the undertaker.

Then he told me and Fence to come in the office.

91

Inside we told him the whole story from the time we'd left Dodge.

I told him I had killed Moore as his pistol was coming to bear on me.

"And Douglas?" he asked.

"As much as I'd like to say I killed him too, I can't. He had me dead to rights with a gun pointed at my back and Fence shot him. Tell him why Fence,"

When Fence was done, Banks said, "well I'll be damned. I was wrong Fence. If you can prove who he really is, the U.S. Government put a price on his head along with any others from the Lawrence raid years ago."

"We're not wanting any money," said Fence. "It was justice we wanted and now we got it. If we're done Sheriff," said Fence, "I think I'll go have a beer."

"Come on," said Banks, "I'll set 'em for us all."

"Thanks," I said, "but first there's a pretty girl I'm going to see."

"She is at that," said Sheriff Banks.

At the hotel I asked for her room number and went up. I knocked on the door and heard her ask, "who is it?"

"It's Dan" I said.

That door opened so fast, I thought it was coming off

the hinges and she came into my arms.

"I've been so worried," she gushed. "When you were gone so long, I thought you were dead. I have a surprise for you, but I want to wait until we get back to the ranch."

"We can go first thing in the morning, if you want," I said.

"You mean?" she started, but stopped.

Shaking my head I said, "it's over Lily. You never have to worry about them again."

92

Fence wanted to hang around Dodge for a little while, but promised he'd be home in a few days.

The closer we got to the ranch, the happier she was. We were no sooner in the door than she pulled that envelope out of her bag. She handed it to me to read it myself. It was from a lawyer's office in Wichita.

"I thought it was a letter from your mother," I said.

"It is," she said, "in a way. Mother did make it to town that day. She went straight to her lawyer. She told him to take David's name off of everything to do with the ranch. She also told him that she thought he had followed her to town and that she was afraid for her life and mine. Now I know for sure that he killed her. I believe he waited outside of town for her and when she started home, he spooked her horse in some way making it throw her off."

"Anyway like you said, it's over now. What are you going to do with this place?" I asked. Afraid she was going to say, sell it and move away.

"Stay right here," she said.

"So we'll be neighbors," I said.

"I was hoping more like partners," said Lily.

"I was hoping so too," I told her, "but not in the ranch business."

She looked at me confused.

"I was hoping you'd be my partner in life, not just a ranch," I told. "Will you marry me Lily?"

"It's what I've hoped for since the day I met you in the diner," she said, and I kissed her.